TUSCAN
Enchantment

TUSCAN
Enchantment

Antonia goes to Tuscany to rebuild her life. The last thing she wants to do
is fall in love, least of all with rich, arrogant, aristocratic Lorenzo.

Kate Zarrelli

Romaunce Books

First published by Romaunce Books in 2023
Suite 2, Top Floor, 7 Dyer Street, Cirencester, Gloucestershire, GL7 2PF

Tuscan Enchantment

Paperback ISBN 9781739117313

Cover design and content by Ray Lipscombe
Printed and bound in Great Britain

Romaunce Books™ is a registered trademark

For Wendie

This was no cold marble – this was a man! Antonia goes to Tuscany to rebuild her life. The last thing she wants to do is fall in love, least of all with rich, arrogant, aristocratic Lorenzo.

Librarian Antonia Gray has fled England for northern Tuscany after an unhappy love affair to work on the archive of a seventeenth-century Italian explorer, a member of a centuries-old aristocratic family. There she meets his descendant, Lorenzo Quattromani, rich, arrogant, handsome – and engaged to the beautiful and ruthless Giselle. The last thing Antonia wants is to fall in love, least of all with someone so dangerous. His engagement, though, is not what it seems, and Lorenzo breaks down Antonia's resistance. But Giselle has other ideas.

Tuscan Enchantment
Kate Zarrelli

Chapter One

Lunigiana, northern Tuscany, 2019

For a moment Antonia thought that she was once more in England, the England she had come away to forget.

Glossy thoroughbred horses grazed in the paddock, the hedgerows were lush and green and a riot of wild flowers nodded their heads in the gentle breeze that softened the heat of the day. But it was a rainy spring which had given Tuscany a freshness unusual for an afternoon in early July.

'Antonia!'

The old imperious voice cut through her thoughts. It was a voice accustomed to unquestioning obedience. This was no surprise. Antonia's employer, Laura, Countess Quattromani, was at eighty-four one of the last of an illustrious noble line. Her coat of arms, four hands held uncompromisingly palm forward, crumbled above the portals of many a ruined castle dotted about the beautiful landscape.

As Antonia turned in the direction of the voice, her illusion of an English landscape vanished. Pale gold in the afternoon sunlight, the countess's three-hundred-year-old villa had as its backdrop rows of vines climbing up into the foothills of the imposing Apuan Alps. In contrast to their rough majesty was the formal garden in front of the villa, with its topiary hedges in the shape of dragons and lions and the pretty splashing fountain with a smiling bronze Cupid as its centrepiece.

The countess was standing before this fountain, looking anything but pleased.

'Guests!' she exclaimed. 'We've got guests here disturbing our peace!' The old lady's bony hand shook as she grasped the shiny knob of her walking stick, then waved it in the air.

In the three months Antonia had been at the villa, she had never seen the countess so annoyed. Eccentric, yes, and a demanding person to work for, but never angry.

'And I was so looking forward to getting on with Gianluca's papers this afternoon!' she added crossly. 'I suppose we'll just have to put up with them!'

'Your guests won't have come to see me,' said Antonia gently. 'I can continue where we left off earlier, and make notes of anything I need to check with you.'

Laura Quattromani's face softened. 'You dear girl. You really are a treasure.' The countess's English was almost perfect, learned in London when she was a child during the war. Because of her father's political views, he had thought it safer to send the family into exile, while he continued to help and shelter partisans at home. As the countess had explained, even a London threatened by the Blitz was a more secure place for the Quattromanis than staying in Italy.

Although the countess talked about Gianluca Quattromani as if he was a dear cousin, he had in fact died centuries ago, after a career consolidating an already vast family fortune by trading with the Far East along the routes established by Marco Polo. But this afternoon the old lady was going to have to put aside Gianluca's adventures, which came alive in his letters and diaries, as a silver Mercedes was now drawing up on the gravelled forecourt of the villa.

As Antonia watched nervously, the most glamorous couple she had ever seen stepped out of it. Feeling awkward and insignificant, she tried to move away, but the old lady's restraining hand on her arm stopped her.

'It gives me great pleasure to introduce my nephew, Lorenzo Quattromani,' barked the countess. 'My companion and librarian, Antonia Gray.'

Antonia shook the warm, strong hand offered her, but after her first glance could barely summon the courage to look again at its owner's face. Her mouth was dry as she mum-bled a greeting, and she was aware of a flush creeping up her neck under her pale tan. Italy was full of perfectly ordinary men who managed to look like gods, but this was clearly no ordinary man, and he outshone them all. Lorenzo Quattromani was utterly beautiful, and no doubt he knew it, Antonia thought miserably. He was one of those infuriating men who always seemed cucumber cool whatever the weather, and Antonia was painfully conscious that she must have been looking hot, bothered and very scruffy in the old canvas overall she wore for her work in the dust and mould of the Quattromani library. Unable to raise her eyes, she looked straight in front of her, only to see the shadowed hollow of his throat, the strong column of his neck. Lorenzo was tall, at least six foot two to her five foot six, his shoulders square but not heavy, his waist narrow and taut, it seemed to her, under the fine fabric of his crisp linen shirt. His skin was golden – there was no other way to describe it – his hair black and gently curling. Her gaze dropped downwards in embarrassment. Dark trousers, also of linen, expensively casual, which on any other man would have looked merely crumpled and weary, encased slim hips.

How at ease he is with himself, and he must know I'm not! Her flush deepened as she remembered a long-forgotten incident from her school days. Charlotte Gardner, the most daring girl in the school, had returned from a holiday in Florence declaring that Italian men had the narrowest hips in the world. As if he was reading her thoughts, Antonia heard Lorenzo's easy, mocking laughter, and despite herself looked up into his face with a small stab of anger. She caught sight of a classic Roman nose and chiselled lips curled in laughter, revealing strong white teeth.

Go on, then, make fun of me!

Angry now, she glared into eyes that were a startling slate grey in the warm olive tones of his face. It was these eyes,

4

as much as his mockery and the lithe perfection of his body, that tightened the muscles of Antonia's throat and made her more tongue-tied than ever.

'Do park that car round the back,' exclaimed his aunt. 'Anyone would think we were new money to look at it!'

'Oh, Aunt!' he laughed. 'Ms Gray – that is, Miss, surely? This is my fiancée, Giselle Landsdorf. She is a buyer for Sotheby's in London – the art auctioneer – perhaps you know them?'

Patronising, aren't we! But Antonia was too polite to say anything. Inevitably, a man like Lorenzo had to have a beautiful and sophisticated companion. As tall as he, Giselle was fair where he was dark. She looked to Antonia to be about twenty-five, *the same age as me but so different,* so perhaps five years younger than her lover. Her long, straw-coloured hair contrasted with the light coffee tone of her skin and the hazel of her eyes. She could have been a model. Giselle did not bother to greet Antonia, but simply looked her dismissively up and down with a glimmer of a smirk.

Antonia, with her dusting of freckles across her nose, her untameable chestnut-brown hair constantly working its way out of its ribbon, knew she could not compare with this girl's elegance.

The countess, meanwhile, had summoned her butler, the dignified and respectful Luigi, and was making arrangements for lunch to be served. As Luigi bowed and withdrew, he shot Antonia a quick, almost furtive look of sympathy and encouragement. She smiled back. Although the old lady was kind to her and admired her work and professionalism, Antonia knew that, like Luigi, she was paid to be there, and this pair wouldn't let her forget it. She told herself not to be so sensitive, but felt strongly that although she would eat the same food at the same table as they did, she could only be a source of amusement to this beautiful couple, a sort of modern court jester, an opportunity for them to show off their faultless English and their cosmopolitanism. The meal over, she would go back to work, while they went to amuse themselves. Yes, she had understood the snigger, the condescension in the almond eyes of Giselle Landsdorf. Nevertheless, she put her thoughts aside as they moved into the coolness of the villa and took their seats at the mahogany table in the main dining room.

'Why do you always eat in here, Aunt? There is space here for twenty diners!' said Lorenzo.

'It would make a perfect conference room,' added Giselle.

'Well, it isn't,' retorted Laura Quattromani. 'I know what you're getting at, but for as long as I am alive it will be what my ancestors intended – a place for the family to eat.'

There was an awkward silence, in which Antonia saw the couple exchange glances, Giselle raising her eyes heavenwards. No doubt the dining room had seen more splendid, lively days, but Antonia loved the place just as it was. No matter how light her footsteps, they could always be heard on the cool Carrara marble floor. Even the faintest of breezes lifted the voile curtains, and the tarnished old mirrors in gilt frames gave her reflection an ethereal, mystical quality, as of a bygone age. Antonia could not help but wonder at all the people who must have gazed at themselves in these mirrors throughout the villa's long history. What had been their hopes, their fears, their joys? Oh, how long would this sneering pair stay here? Long enough to spoil things.

Luigi was busily serving the vichyssoise from a silver soup tureen into porcelain dishes bearing the crest of the Quattromani family. The same crest was etched on the silver rings holding crisply starched linen napkins, fresh at every meal. The countess uttered a rapid grace – Antonia noticed that the visitors did not join in. She raised her gaze from her plate only to find that those extraordinary slate-grey eyes staring right back at her.

'And what brings you to my aunt's villa? I can't imagine it's the company,' said Lorenzo, his drawl a mixture of curiosity and boredom. At the other end of the table the countess gave a sharp grunt of annoyance. Antonia refused to rise to the bait, and answered him truthfully, if a little tremulously, hoping she did not sound too defensive.

'I am cataloguing the Quattromani papers. I am a qualified librarian, and this is a unique professional opportunity.'

Instead of answering her straightaway, Lorenzo threw back his head and laughed, a low, rich laugh that she was clearly not meant to join in. Instead, to her horror, she felt a stab of fleeting desire, a desire that made her long to kiss his exposed neck, to savour the musky scent of his olive skin. Not only was this man laughing at her so rudely, but he also seemed to know the effect he was having on her.

'Well,' he sneered, 'I suppose I ought to be grateful I'm not a librarian, stuck away with all my aunt's musty papers. And what, may I ask, were the sort of professional opportunities you had before you came here?'

Antonia thought it best just to soldier on.

'I worked in a public library in Somerset,' she answered simply. 'I loved that job – I loved the readers, and my colleagues were kind.' Their faces swam before her eyes now. Mr. Bennett, the head librarian, who had always seemed to her like a favourite uncle, had that knack of reading her every mood. He knew that she was leaving before she announced it, and he understood why. She still burned with the shame of what had driven her away from the little town, though none of what happened had been her fault. Being made a fool of is so hard to talk about sometimes.

'Hello? Are you still with us, Ms Gray?'

'Oh! I beg your pardon.' But Lorenzo had already turned away and was muttering something to his fiancée that Antonia didn't hear – the girl laughed into her napkin. Antonia looked down at her dish, her face hot, and lost herself again in her memories.

Friends had tried to congratulate her on her decision to go abroad. 'Italy? But how romantic!' they'd exclaimed, when romance was quite definitely the last thing on Antonia's mind. 'It'll be a wonderful new start, just the thing you need!' Only Arthur Bennett had kissed her forehead and said, 'Remember, little one, you can run away as far as you like, but your heartache will always be with you, until you finally tell it to go away. You can't run away from yourself.'

Sitting there at Laura Quattromani's table, so many miles away, Antonia felt tears well up, when she had thought she could not possibly cry anymore. In that small town she had felt she had known everybody, and that they had cared about her. Here instead she was a nobody, with this diabolically handsome man laughing at her while his beautiful companion indifferently examined her own immaculate French manicure. She was jolted back to the present when he spoke to her again: 'Well, yes, I can see that even the company of my aunt might be a welcome diversion.'

'That's enough of your sarcasm, Lorenzo,' rapped out his aunt. 'Miss Gray is my employee and should not be treated as a source of amusement for you. What brings you here anyway?'

'Giselle leaves on Monday for a month's assignment in New York. I've put the Gavedo estates into the factor's hands for the time being, and thought I might pass a month's holiday here. Perhaps I'll be able to amuse your precious Ms Gray, that's if you'll allow her any time off,' he answered. 'Please can I take her to the seaside?' he added in an infuriating mock-baby voice.

'Bah! You take nothing seriously!' barked the countess. 'I'm telling you now that I'm leaving this villa to the City of Florence. I know they'll take better care of it than you ever would. Miss Gray is here expressly to put all of the family archive in order. That way I'll at least be able to die in peace! And another thing, if you want to stay here a whole month, although I can't imagine why, since you find my company so dull, I'd be grateful if you would not mention the Gavedo estates again.'

'But Aunt,' began Giselle in a wheedling tone, 'what about the Quattromani Foundation? A conference and cultural centre in your name would be famous throughout Europe.'

'The Landsdorf Foundation, you mean. Something for you to do when you get bored of travelling. You could have set up something like that back in Switzerland had you wanted to. And I'm not your aunt. You're not married to him yet, you know. Sometimes I must be grateful for small mercies,' retorted the countess.

Antonia felt a surge of affection towards her crotchety employer. The countess had led her to believe that she was the last of her line. Clearly, she had not wanted to admit to the existence of this spoiled, lazy nephew and his selfish, grasping girlfriend. Antonia had no family of her own, though she wished fervently that she did, but she could see why the old lady did not claim her own relatives. Why, Antonia wondered, had the countess herself never married and had a family? As it was, perhaps her title would pass to Lorenzo, although his aunt was clearly bent on ensuring that he would not inherit all the Quattromani lands. Though Laura Quattromani was now an elderly lady, it was obvious that she had been a beautiful woman. Even now she was elegant and imposing, with her high, aristocratic cheekbones, her dark, arched eyebrows, and her abundant, now-white hair wound back into a neat chignon.

You're not married to him yet, the countess had said to Giselle. And yet, what a beautiful ice-maiden of a bride the Swiss girl would make. Theirs would be the kind of society wedding that would feature in all the European editions of *Vogue*. Perhaps one day she would see their faces again in a well-thumbed magazine she would pick up in her dentist's waiting-room.

Antonia was torn from these thoughts by the arrival of the next course, ribbons of pasta made in the cellar kitchens of the villa, the sauce made from the mushrooms which grew wild in the woods at the end of the paddock. Giselle, however, was pushing her plate away, her perfect nose wrinkling in scorn, her fine lips compressed with anger. The countess's words had struck home. Lorenzo, on the other hand, seemed merely amused at the exchange between the two women. Certainly it did not affect his appetite, for he devoured his food with an enthusiasm which was in marked contrast to Giselle's disdain. At least he wasn't such a snob that he cannot eat simple, local food, Antonia thought.

The meal came to an end, with Giselle merely picking at her plate. Antonia wondered if this was how the beautiful Swiss girl kept her elegant figure, shown to its best advantage in a fine lawn blouse, narrow capri pants and soft Gucci loafers.

As she sat there, far from home, Antonia seemed to hear her mother saying to her, 'Just one of those silly girls obsessed with her food. There's nothing like a good appetite and taking a nice long walk for staying healthy and happy.' But her mother had been unable in the end to do anything to save her own health. She would never hear her mother's no-nonsense words again. Cancer had seen to that two years before, the poor woman worn out by bringing up her child alone, sacrificing everything for her. *I'm just glad she never saw what drove me away from the place and the people I loved.* Antonia made a great effort to pull herself together, refusing to let the tears that pricked at her eyes to spill out in front of this spoiled and self-centred couple who cared nothing about her. That man would probably think he'd upset me himself, and she wouldn't give him or his condescending girlfriend that satisfaction!

Antonia resolved to take her mother's advice right now and go for a walk around the estate.

'I would like to get some fresh air before going back to Gianluca. Shall we meet again in the library at four?' she said to the countess.

'An excellent idea, Antonia. I'm sure you'll find your

own company infinitely better than what you'll find here,' answered the old lady, with a glance of undisguised disapproval at her uninvited guests. Antonia nodded briefly towards Giselle, who ignored her completely, and at the infuriating Lorenzo, who just smiled and winked at her.

'Impossible man!' she muttered under her breath as she left the room.

Antonia adored these brief times she had to herself. She had been so often alone in her life that she had grown used to her own company. For each walk she took around the villa's estates she would set herself a different goal, another corner to explore, another path to take through the olive groves, another tumble-down farm building to share with nobody but the tiny scuttling lizards.

Today, wearing a little straw hat with a white scarf tied over it against the heat of the sun, she set off along a path leading up into one of the gentler foothills of the mountains. The day was hot and still. The breeze had dropped and barely a breath of air disturbed the grass. Even the lizards seemed to have gone to sleep. Birds twittered lazily in the olive trees and in the hedgerows, as if they knew that the countess had banned hunting them on her land. Antonia heard distant cow-bells. How distant she couldn't guess, as sounds travelled so far on such a day.

The path climbed gently upwards until it was met by another track along a small summit, from which Antonia looked down into another lush valley. The cross-roads was marked by a little stone building which Antonia at first took to be an old shelter before she realised that it was in fact a tiny chapel. She stepped into its mossy coolness, glad for a moment to be out of the sun. On the far wall she glimpsed a little marble plaque and went forward to look at it. It was a delicate carving of the Virgin Mary and the baby Jesus, centuries old, but not forgotten by the people who worked in the olive groves. She found three fresh lilies in a pot below the plaque. Antonia drank in their scent, closing her eyes as she did so.

She did not immediately realise that the interior of the little chapel had grown dark. She turned around, and could not hold back her gasp of fear and surprise. Yet the man who blocked her way was no stranger.

'You followed me!'

Lorenzo Quattromani did not reply. She could not make out his expression because the light was behind him, and so was totally unprepared for what happened next. He strode up to her, seized her shoulders and pushed her gently but firmly against the wall of the chapel. The little hat and scarf were knocked from her head and her chestnut curls fell about her shoulders. She felt the sudden coldness of the rough stones of the wall through the thin fabric of her cotton dress – and shoved him back.

'What the hell are you playing at?'

He put his hands up, but Antonia couldn't tell if this was a way of saying sorry, or if he thought her unreasonable. *I don't care what he thinks anyway.*

'You think because you're lord of the manor, or will be one day, that you can do as you like with the serfs? Nice way to treat your girlfriend too.'

To her surprise Lorenzo moved away at once, to lean against the opposite wall. He wouldn't meet her eyes.

'I don't care if you tell her,' he said quietly.

'Your business, not mine. But I suppose I'll have to look for another job now, thanks to you.'

He turned to look at her then. 'Don't do that, Antonia – please. It mightn't seem that way, but I am very fond of my aunt. The work you are doing for her – it means everything to her. She's really pleased to have found you. She told me so, the moment you were out of earshot. And what's more, she warned me off you.'

'Nice that she felt she had to,' retorted Antonia.

'I'm not very good at doing what I'm told,' he said, looking away again. 'Probably because most of the time I get to do what I want. But I was – what is the expression? I was out of order. I'm sorry. I mean it. It's just that you're so pretty—'

'Oh, so it's my fault is it? Keep digging, Mr Quattromani.'

'I'd better go. I'm only making things worse. Your poor hat…' He picked it up, dusted it down, and handed it to her. 'I promise not to jump on you like that again. God knows what you must have thought. But you resisted me. Most of the women I encounter don't—'

'What towering arrogance!' said Antonia. 'Yes, I think you had better go.'

'I didn't mean it like that. I meant that most of them are after what they can get, and that's less about me and more about what I own. You, though, you have spirit, little librarian. I didn't expect that.'

'Less of the little, Mr Quattromani. I'm only a head shorter than you. Though I don't think that's what you mean. To be a "little librarian" as you put it, meant getting a decent degree, working to get the right experience for library school and then working hard for a postgraduate qualification. At least your aunt appreciates that. And I'm twenty-five years old. I'm not a kid.'

'I've learnt my lesson. I won't be here much longer – but can I ask you at least to call me Lorenzo?'

'All right, Lorenzo. But would you please leave now.'

'I'm going.'

Then he did something that surprised her almost as much as anything else. He knelt and gathered up the lilies, as the vase had been knocked over in their struggle, and the blooms were trampled and bruised. He eased the broken flowers back into the vase, then straightened up and walked slowly out into the sunlight without another word.

Chapter Two

Antonia stood rooted to the spot, thinking about his tender handling of the broken flowers. A little warning voice, her own instinct for self-preservation, told her *beware*. Seeing this other side of his personality made Lorenzo in some ways a far more dangerous man than the one who had tried to kiss her. She peered slowly round the entrance of the chapel to see Lorenzo retreating along the path to the left. A moment later his tall figure was concealed by the hedgerow at a turn in the path. Antonia took a deep breath, her heart still racing, and set off straight ahead, back down towards the villa, her footsteps faltering only slightly.

Nobody must know. But why did he do it? Is it to get back at his aunt because I'm her employee and she was sharp with him at the dinner table? How childish! Or is it something to do with Giselle? She rounded the front of the villa and came upon the girl, stretched out on a sun-lounger in a white bikini chosen to make the most of her perfect figure and even tan. Giselle could have been asleep, for her Versace sunglasses gave nothing away, except that her feet tapped idly in time to whatever she was plugged into on her cell phone, and her slender fingers enclosed her nearly empty glass. Antonia hurried past, hoping Giselle would think her flushed face was due to running. She caught a glimpse of her own startled expression mirrored in the black pools of the sunglasses.

'Hey there! Angela!'

Antonia stopped, turning round. 'It's Antonia.'

'Oh yes, so it is. Get me another of these would you?' said Giselle, waving the glass idly.

'Pardon?' said Antonia, not believing her ears.

'Campari, not too much ice.'

Antonia remembered Lorenzo's words, *You have spirit, little librarian.*

'I'm sure you can manage that yourself,' she heard herself say.

Giselle simply smirked. 'Where've you been, then? You look a bit... damp,' she said.

Antonia felt cold despite the heat of the day. *Is this something those two have cooked up between them? I can just imagine it. Make that little librarian fall in love with you. Let's see how deep her English cool really is! Then he laughs in that flippant way of his, and looks for his chance. And what do I? I give it to him, telling everyone I'm going out for walk on my own!*

Luigi saved the day, crossing the gravel in front of her, carrying another Campari on a tray. 'I thought you might be ready for another one, Miss Landsdorf,' he said, the impeccable servant always anticipating a need. Then he looked at Antonia. 'Is everything all right?' he asked with discreet concern.

'Oh, yes, just the heat! I'm fine, really. Thank you!'

Get a grip! Lorenzo doesn't care, perhaps not even about Giselle. All he cares about is amusing himself. Just make sure you're not alone with him again, you idiot!

Hoping not to meet anyone else, she flitted quietly up the marble staircase to her rooms in the attic of the villa.

'Sanctuary!' she said aloud when she reached the part of the villa that had been the servants' quarters. Now the only estate employees who lived in were Luigi and his wife Elena, lodged in a separate converted stable block. The other four employees all came in each day from the nearest village, now that the kitchens of the villa had acquired all the modern labour-saving devices that made unnecessary the many servants of days gone by.

The rich, dark mahogany furniture in her rooms was of a kind that Antonia had only gazed at in the windows of antique shops at home, preferably when they were closed and she couldn't be tempted. The chest of drawers and the dressing table were topped with cool slabs of delicately veined Carrara marble, while the doors of the wardrobe were inlaid with tiny pieces of mother of pearl forming a floral pattern. Inset into the great wrought-iron head of the double bed was a tiny circular painting of a landscape with a ruined castle, no doubt one of the castles of the Quattromani family, while the bed itself was covered by a lovely lace counterpane, worked by a former housekeeper of the family. Attached to the ceiling above the bed was a frame on which a gossamer-thin mosquito net was looped. Antonia had already had reason to be grateful for the presence of the net. Hungry insects were the only drawback of the warm and balmy summer nights. All these beautifully crafted things had seemed to welcome Antonia when she had arrived three months earlier, but now they seemed to represent a life that she could never be a part of.

Closing the door of her little apartment, she crossed the cool floor of glazed terracotta to the windows looking out on the formal gardens at the front of the villa.

Her bedroom was adjoined by a marble-lined bathroom on one side and by a little sitting room on the other, opening out onto a beautiful roof-top terrace where Antonia could sit and sunbathe in privacy. She decided to go and sit in a deckchair until her heart stopped pounding. But as she passed her dressing table she caught sight of her reflection in its oval mirror, and gasped. No wonder Giselle had smirked!

Her hair was a mess, her ribbon coming loose, but that was the least of her problems. The simple cotton dress she had ironed so crisply was now crumpled and had a button missing. Turning her back to the mirror and craning her head round, she saw to her horror that the white fabric was smeared with moss from the wall of the chapel. But even if the Swiss girl had missed her dirtied clothes, Antonia's face would have given the game away. Her blue eyes were wide and frightened, like the eyes of a cornered wild animal, which was exactly how she felt. She pulled a brush rapidly through her unruly and resisting hair, and could not help a little spurt of pride at its healthy bounce and shine before she tidied it back into its ribbon. She then swiftly changed her dress.

Out on the terrace, she flopped into a deckchair, turning her face up to the sun and shutting her eyes to hear the birdsong better. Despite the excitement of the afternoon, she fell asleep within minutes, waking up three-quarters of an hour later feeling much more composed.

Time to go back to work! She headed downstairs towards the library. The countess would have finished her siesta by now and would be ready for another good spell of work amongst the Quattromani papers.

In fact, when Antonia entered the long galleried chamber of the library, with its distinctive smell of old leather bindings and beeswax polish, the countess was already there. Antonia felt guilty, as if she had deserted her post. Laura Quattromani raised her head from where she sat at the long central table, between piles of books and manuscripts, and to Antonia's relief spoke kindly. 'You've had a proper rest, for once. Now where were we, my dear?'

'Gianluca's correspondence with Doria's agent in Genoa, about the bales of Mandarin silk,' Antonia replied, her confidence gradually returning as she found herself back on her own professional ground. She knew that people like Lorenzo and Giselle would have no interest in this, so she and the countess could be sure of working undisturbed.

'Let's continue with the bills of sale from March 1602,' suggested Antonia as she opened the laptop which perched incongruously amongst all these leather and vellum relics of a less hurried age. The countess had told her an internet connection was only installed in anticipation of Antonia's arrival, so that the work she was doing could be linked with research libraries and academics around the world. It made her feel that she was part of something bigger, that she and the countess were not working alone.

The afternoon's tasks went on, with the sorting of Gianluca Quattromani's correspondence into the acid-free folders, which would save them from any further ravages of time, and the transcription of his elegantly sloping sepia hand-writing that would mean eventually his archive could be published on the internet and make his extraordinary story available to scholars all over the world. Antonia wondered for a moment if anyone who would read Gianluca's correspondence in years to come would think of the efforts of a humble librarian in making it available to them. *It's a shame that Gianluca's last male descendant seems to have no interest in his adventures.* As she became absorbed in her work, however, the incidents of that afternoon began to seem only like the hazy memory of a bad dream. With an afternoon's good solid work behind her, Antonia felt much stronger about facing Lorenzo again.

Lorenzo himself strolled into the dining room as though nothing had happened.

'Good evening, Antonia. *Buonasera*, Aunt,' he said, and sat down to eat. Giselle swept in a moment later.

Even here, where there's nobody she needs to impress, she has to make an entrance, Antonia thought. Giselle had exchanged the capri pants for a deceptively simple, exquisitely cut grey silk sheath dress, which rippled across her sleek body as she crossed the candlelit room. The dress itself was designed to command attention, and could not fail to do so on a shape like hers. However, to Antonia's amazement, Lorenzo simply ignored Giselle, refusing to lift his focus from his plate. Throughout the meal he did not speak to her directly. He did not even need to ask her to pass him things on the table, which in a simpler household might have broken the deadlock, because the ever-attentive Luigi anticipated every need of the four diners.

Have they had a row?

Antonia caught sight of the countess looking at them furtively, with just a touch of malice. Despite the delicate flavours of Elena's excellent cooking, Antonia did not enjoy the meal. *You could cut the atmosphere with a knife.* The Swiss girl was doing all she could to attract Lorenzo's attention. She tossed back her hair, pouted her beautiful, sulky mouth provocatively, and crossed and re-crossed her legs beneath the table so that no one could fail to hear the suggestive whispering of the silk dress against her bronzed thighs. Lorenzo refused to react. There was little noise in the room other than the chink of silver cutlery on porcelain and Luigi's measured tread as he went back and forth, his spotless linen napkin as always across his forearm. Antonia sneaked a look at him, wondering what effect Giselle's display was having on the only other man in the room, but his impassive face gave nothing away. The meal seemed to go on forever. She was glad, however, that the twilight and the flickering light of the candles on the table helped to disguise the anxiety she was sure was showing on her face. I'd love to go back to the library, but I can't keep running away from trouble.

Antonia stood up as soon as it was polite to do so. Luigi had already cleared the table and gone back to the kitchen. 'Good night, everybody,' she said, with forced cheerfulness. Turning to the countess she said, 'I think I shall go back to the library for a while.'

'And I think you should have an evening off, my dear,' replied the old lady.

Antonia felt a sudden impulse to hug the countess, but she was sure it wasn't the done thing. 'Yes, perhaps I will. It's been quite a tiring day.'

Giselle ignored her, but to Antonia's surprise, Lorenzo got up from the table and opened the door for her. He inclined his head slightly and said 'I hope you have a pleasant evening, Antonia.'

'Oh … thank you.'

Up in her rooms, she crossed to the window. It was an exquisite evening, and tomorrow would be another glorious day. The sky was a dusky pink darkening to purple on the horizon, against which stood tall cypress trees, like sentinels guarding the estate. Crickets chirped without stopping, and although it was still early, fireflies already flashed back and forth. Antonia stood for some moments drinking in the beauty of the scene.

I'm not going to let anything or anyone spoil this for me. She loosened the fine mesh of the mosquito net above her bed before turning on the bedside light. It was the least she could do to keep these particular predators away from her fresh English skin.

Antonia tried to relax by reading a few pages of an Ian Rankin novel she'd found amongst the countess's books before she turned out the light, but gave up the attempt when she found herself reading the same page for the third time. She normally loved crime stories, and prided herself on being able to follow Inspector Rebus's train of thought to the same solution. She thought of herself as a kind of detective in her own work for the countess, piecing together the adventures of Gianluca Quattromani from the scanty clues he left about himself in his letters. Her organised, methodical mind was able to look back, put together the right bits of information to chart the course of Gianluca's journeys and business dealings, just as Rebus himself followed the thread of a motive, discarding all the red herrings as he went on.

Antonia sighed and shut the book, stretching herself out in her comfortable bed. Everything today had changed so suddenly, from the moment the silver Mercedes had arrived with its two passengers. The villa was the same, as timeless as ever, the countess had not changed, nor had their work. Yet Antonia suddenly felt terribly alone and homesick for the first time since coming to Italy. Running away had lost its charm. She shut her eyes, curled up on her side, and tried to think of home, not home as it was when she left so quickly, nor the dark and seedy Edinburgh streets walked by Rebus, but an idealised Britain of times gone by. She imagined the one the countess might have known as a child, in which men wore hats and opened the doors of elegant Wolseley cars for ladies who curled their hair and had seamed stockings, or because it was wartime painted their legs that way.

She woke up an hour later, having fallen asleep in her clothes, the bedside light still on, and got up to shower away the day.

Far below Antonia's rooms was the exquisite chamber occupied by Lorenzo and Giselle, decorated with delicate Chinese hand-painted wallpaper brought back by another roving Quattromani in the nineteenth century. The oriental style of the room was enhanced by its rare and ornate furniture with filigree carving and shell inlay. The bed, by contrast, was large, modern and as simple as anything to come out of contemporary Japan. Its clean lines, however, helped to emphasise the intricacy and craftsmanship of the rest of the room. While he had admired the furnishings, as he always did, when he arrived, all this meant nothing in that moment to Lorenzo.

Beneath the mosquito net draped around the bed, Lorenzo's head was thrown back, his eyes shut tight, his mouth slightly open as his body thrust rhythmically back and forth between the raised hips of Giselle Landsdorf. Her long legs were twined around him, but every now and then she would raise her smooth bronzed thighs higher and press them around him, inflaming his need to penetrate her even more deeply. He paused for a moment and grasped one ankle after another, flinging them up onto his shoulders. Her blond locks were splayed about the pillows, a contrast to his ruffled raven-black hair. He felt her nails drag down the skin of his chest, but he gave no sign of the pain. As Lorenzo moved faster and harder her animal cries became stronger. Their lovemaking was all fierce passion, with no room for tenderness. With a low moan, Lorenzo finished servicing the beautiful Swiss girl.

His frenzy over, Lorenzo arched his back and shoulders for a moment like a great cat stretching. He withdrew from Giselle almost immediately, rolling over to lie face up at the other side of the bed. He did not bother to cover up his nakedness, but lay there breathing deeply. Giselle had turned away equally quickly to curl up with her back to him, but she did pull up the linen sheet to cover herself.

Lorenzo sighed.

What I've just done is more like what the stallion does when he's brought to the mare. All that was missing was to have the stablehands there to supervise us! The world thinks we're perfectly matched, of course, and that just make me feel worse. He turned onto his side. *We're both successful, whatever that means. She's a rising star in the auction house and I'm making a real go of managing these estates – exactly what a First in Land Economy from Cambridge qualifies me to do.* He listened to Giselle's regular breathing. *Her appetite's satisfied, anyway. She's fast asleep. Look at us! We should be cradled in each other's arms, like lovers are meant to be, or talking perhaps. But I don't think we've even got anything to say to each other.*

Lorenzo shifted about but could not get comfortable. Finally, he swung his legs to one side and stood up. The room was grey in the moonlight, and in the long mirror on the armoire he could see the play of the shadows emphasising the tautness of the muscles of his thighs and calves and the hard flatness of his stomach. The dark power of his manhood was now quiet, at least for a while. Lorenzo stepped as lightly and stealthily as a panther across the marble floor to the window. He looked out at the topiary hedges and the immaculately kept flowerbeds, and heard the gentle tinkle of the little Cupid fountain. He sighed. He knew he would not sleep now, in spite of his recent burst of energy. His feeling of dissatisfaction would not leave him. *We've been together a couple of years now, less because of all those business trips. Yup, she's got beauty, brains, style. And me? I'm her stud, and the next stage in her career trajectory. Break from her international career? It's in her diary. Become the director of her own cultural foundation? That too. Marry me. Check! Only my aunt is standing in her way because she won't let her have the villa.* He ground his teeth. *I was going to restore the ruined castle at Gavedo so she could have that instead, but oh no, that wouldn't do. 'Too remote,' she said.*

Lorenzo sighed. He could not share these misgivings with anyone. His friends would not understand. They thought he and Giselle were the perfect couple. In fact, they envied him.

I might have been able to talk to Antonia. With her unruly hair and dreamy face, she reminded him of those pre-Raphaelite paintings. *But I've messed that up all right! The flash in her eyes, though! Who would have thought that gentle exterior hid such fire and determination? Not a bit like the rich English girls at Cambridge balls.* As he pondered, he realised Antonia was unlike anyone he had ever met, at least as far as he could remember.

It was true what he had said to her. Women did not resist him. He had been occasionally unfaithful to Giselle when she was away on a buying trip. He always excused his behaviour to himself by calling it a necessary release. Besides, he had always made a point of never waking up beside his conquests, so they counted as nothing but casual encounters. He would slip away in the darkness of a San Moritz winter morning or in the pale pink of a Monte Carlo dawn. He always took precautions and those girls always got as good as they gave. He smiled wryly at one memory, a young Frenchwoman recently married to a German nobleman in his seventies. If she behaved with her old husband with the passion she had shown to her Italian lover she would soon be a widow and sole mistress of Schloss Waldstein and its accompanying Moselle vineyards.

Perhaps I should have stayed in touch. He quickly forgot the thought. He did wonder occasionally if Giselle was faithful to him, but realised he did not really care all that much as long as her adventures did not take place under his nose. He knew they were not in love, whatever that meant, but he also knew that they suited each other.

He glanced at the bed, realising that not only was he not sleepy, but that he had been thinking subconsciously about Giselle as if she was one of his casual adventures – he didn't particularly need to wake up beside her. He slipped on the linen trousers that were draped over a chair and pushed his feet into a pair of comfortable old deck shoes. *I'll go out for a bit. It might make me sleepy, and it's such a beautiful night.*

At Gavedo he always slept well, but that was because he was always busy. He went to bed there with a sense of achievement, a feeling of satisfaction that he had single-handedly turned Quattromani wines from a small local business into a profitable international brand. The white Gavedo grape, a venerable Trebbiano, was now in demand in the most chic restaurants of Manhattan, Mayfair and Milan, but had lost none of its exclusivity and quality. Even without the vineyards, the olive and fig crops surrounding the old castle would have kept him occupied, though not rich. *I play hard, but I work hard, so why won't Aunt take me seriously?*

Laura was his closest living relative since his parents had died in a freak accident in a private jet fifteen years earlier. Lorenzo had been at an English public school at the time, preparing for A levels and Oxbridge, following an educational tradition established by his great-grandfather. He had not grieved much for his mother and father because he had never really known them. They had sent him away to boarding school when he was seven years old, and whenever he did come home he was cared for by his Irish nanny, Teresa Conroy, the only person he had ever really loved. Nanny Conroy had retired to her native west Cork, but Lorenzo kept faithfully in touch. 'My own wee darlin' boy,' she would call him, even when he was a grown man. Thinking about her, Lorenzo smiled. *How much I'd like your good advice now!* Musing on the strange life he had led as a privileged child, lacking in nothing but the normal everyday love of mother and father, Lorenzo went out of the bedroom, shutting the door soundlessly. He walked slowly downstairs, crossed the marble floor of the entrance of the villa and went out into the gardens.

Antonia meanwhile was sleeping from sheer mental exhaustion, but the tension she had been under was forcing its way out in her dreams.

She was back in her old bedroom in the little house she had rented just off the High Street, five minutes' walk from the library. She was waking up and preparing to dress for the day. As usual, her skirt and blouse were hanging ready for her on the door of the wardrobe, and underwear was in a neat pile on her chest of drawers.

But what was this? Not the comfortable and sensible – yes, she knew it was pretty boring – underwear she usually wore, but a ghastly, slippery nylon black-and-red bra and matching briefs. In the dream the showy garments slithered out of her hands and fell to the floor. She turned round, but against the wardrobe door, in place of her modest work clothes, there was now a black chiffon transparent wrap trimmed with feathers. With a cry she tore at the wrap, meaning to pull it to pieces. Instead it entangled her. Her head and arms were caught in it and she struggled to break free. As she fought with the garment she heard a man's sneering laughter, starting as a low chuckle, but gradually growing louder and louder, mocking her.

Antonia woke up crying to find herself sitting up in bed. She had pulled the mosquito net off its frame, and was still fighting to get free of it. The cruel laughter had stopped ringing in her head. All she could hear now was the silence of the Tuscan night. Even the crickets had ceased their chirping. She knew whose laugh that was. She'd hoped never to hear it again, yet it had followed her even here. It was not the easy, sensuous laugh of Lorenzo Quattromani but the voice of George Barton, the man she had almost married, the man she had run away from in tears.

Chapter Three

George had seemed so straightforward, so dependable, a not-long-qualified local solicitor who was generally thought well of in the little town. That was because they didn't know the real George. Antonia shivered in spite of the mild Italian night. She could still hear her friend, the old school friend who was to have been her only bridesmaid, 'Didn't you find it humiliating having to return the wedding presents, cancel the church, tell all your guests it was all off?'

'No. That was nothing when I thought about what a lucky escape I'd had.'

Her old friend and colleague Arthur Bennett had been the kindest. 'George always seemed to me to be a bit too good to be true. I can't say why that is. Call it instinct if you like.'

'Why didn't you say, Arthur?'

'Would you have listened? You were in love. You'd probably only have defended him more. And what did I have? Only a feeling. You can't speak against a man with no evidence.'

'Oh, I got the evidence, Arthur,' Antonia had said in a

small voice. 'But I don't think I can talk about it yet. Not even with you.'

'Quite right. I think that is very dignified of you. Ladylike.'

George's courtship had been very formal, almost old-fashioned, and this had appealed to Antonia. She recalled the very first time they had spoken, although she already knew who he was. Everybody did in that little town. It made what happened later even harder. 'Might I take you to lunch?'

The voice across the library counter was deep, authoritative, a voice used to giving opinions its owner was sure of. George had a broad, sunburned face, brown, crisp curly hair, and was wearing a patched tweed jacket, corduroy trousers and stout brogues. He'd looked not so much like what he was, a country solicitor on his way to building up a solid clientèle, but more like the astute, no-nonsense farmers that he negotiated with. Much of George's work involved handling the legal aspects of the purchase of lush rolling farming land, or dealing with the settlement of the obscurely worded wills of the old county families. This had been a Saturday, so he had exchanged his usual sober suit for clothes like those his clients wore.

Antonia's gaze met his cold blue eyes for a moment. She had been slightly surprised but secretly flattered. 'Yes, thank you. I'd like that. We close today at one. I shall be free then.'

'I'll come back at one, then.' He'd picked up his books, two detective thrillers and a manual on horse husbandry, and he was gone.

That first lunch had taken place in the old coaching inn, the Royal Oak, across the High Street from the library, a place that resisted all efforts to become a modern gastropub, and thrived as a result. A hearty meal in a five-hundred-year-old tavern, beneath darkened beams, horse-trappings and sporting prints that even an inexpert eye could see were the real thing, was a welcome change from the modest cheese on toast and salad Antonia had planned to eat at home. George seemed genuinely interested in her, probing gently for details of her family, although he too must have known, as did everyone else in the little town, about her mother's tragic death and her father's flight from the family home some years before.

'I don't even know where my father is now, or even if he's still alive,' Antonia murmured, grateful for George's interest.

'So you're really alone in the world?' he'd asked, half-admiringly.

'That's me, little orphan Annie!' she said, laughing. 'But to be honest, living here I don't really feel that way. Everybody is so friendly, I feel that I'm part of a family. It was a real stroke of luck that when I qualified a job came up here as assistant librarian. I could come home again, and I know that's what Mother would have wanted. My time studying in London convinced me that's what I wanted too. A better way to live, a gentler pace of life.'

He'd laughed momentarily at that, then answered, 'Well, it can be a gentler life here, certainly. Sometimes not enough happens. I go to London occasionally, you know, see some friends, perhaps take in a show or two. It's certainly another world there.'

An odd look Antonia could not identify had come into the ice-blue eyes. For a split second she thought of an old film she had once seen on television, late one Saturday night. An outwardly normal man, an upstanding member of the community, had turned into a werewolf as the moon waxed full. The transformation started with a wild glitter in his eyes. Antonia quickly brushed the thought away. Everything about George Barton said reassurance and dependability. Perhaps, she thought, he might invite her one day on one of his London outings. He never did.

'I really admire you for the way you go it alone,' he said.

'Well …' She'd laughed, a little ruefully. 'I haven't really got much choice, but I appreciate your saying that just the same.'

After lunch George had accompanied her to the door of her flat, holding her arm carefully as he saw her across the road, then making a point of walking on the outside along the pavement. Antonia wasn't sure if this was weirdly old-fashioned or just considerate. He and she started to meet regularly for lunch on Saturdays, and then once or twice during the week they went out, driving to the cinema in the county town in his elderly Land Rover or going out to dinner. Eventually her favourite readers started to comment on the fact they were seen together so often. In the eyes of the elderly spinster ladies of their little community George and Antonia were engaged long before this became a fact.

'It is nice to see you two young people so happy together,' commented old Miss Milner when she popped in for her weekly supply of American crime novels. For a sweet little old English lady, Miss Milner had pretty bloodthirsty tastes. Antonia had got very good at judging book jacket blurbs, and made a point of getting to know the styles of all the most popular authors in order to help Miss Milner and her other readers make the right selection. It was this attention to people's personal needs that made Antonia so good at her job. If her readers did not realise she spent hours of her own time reading book reviews, skimming through works good and bad, in order to get the right selections onto the library shelves, they certainly did appreciate the results. Antonia smiled back at the old lady.

'George is certainly very kind,' was all she had replied, blushing slightly as she did so.

'Ah yes, but he must really appreciate you, my dear. It was time he found himself a nice girl, and she would have to be a professional. After all, he's going places. And twenty-seven is a good age for a man to settle down, ' answered the old lady with conviction.

Antonia's blush had deepened at these very obvious insinuations, and she had to control the urge to smile at the unmarried lady's apparent expertise in what made a man marriageable. But Miss Milner was right, of course, George appeared to be a good catch. When she had been at college there had not been many opportunities to date. Most of the students on her course had been girls, and besides, that had been the terrible time when her mother had been ill. Romance had been the last thing on her mind then. She'd nearly given up altogether, but her mother would not hear of her interrupting her studies.

'No, my dearest. I want to be sure that you'll be making a dependable career for yourself. You stick in there. Do it for me,' her mother had insisted, her voice starting to fail her.

Antonia had stuck in there. Working hard and fighting through her tears, she'd passed with flying colours, although her mother had died in the Christmas vacation before her final examinations. As George had said, Antonia was alone in the world. She could do a lot worse than give up her loneliness to be with him.

'I'd like you to meet my mother,' George had announced one Saturday lunchtime after they had been meeting for a couple of months. Antonia realised then what was coming, because George was so formal and correct in everything he did. She thought it odd that in all that time, although he had always been very kind and attentive, he'd never gone further than wanting to kiss her. His kisses had frightened her a bit. They were overpowering, rough, and when he pulled away from her he'd looked slightly drunk. But, as she asked herself, what did she know about what was normal and what was not? It was not as if her own mother and father had had a normal married life, with him going off so early in her own young life.

When Antonia met the widowed Mrs Barton, she began to understand why George had not married earlier. His mother was clearly a difficult woman to please. In a moment of uncharacteristic naughtiness, the thought crossed Antonia's mind that it must have been a relief to Mr Barton senior to die in middle-age.

Mrs Barton's gaunt Victorian house was situated at the edge of the town, as if keeping itself apart from its less imposing neighbours. It looked a bit neglected, with peeling paint and a scruffy front garden, and the dark blinds drawn halfway down the windows gave the place a forbidding aspect. The house seemed to scowl at Antonia, and its occupant was no different.

'So this is the young lady?' barked Mrs Barton, the moment she opened the door.

Antonia felt like a prize calf being prodded in the market place, an item of merchandise. There was no word of welcome.

'Yes, Mother. This is Antonia,' said George quietly.

'Well, you'd better come in then,' rapped out Mrs Barton, sounding as if she would rather they went somewhere else. George's mother wore sensible shoes, thick nylon stockings and a severe old tweed suit, even though it was a mild

September day. Her iron-grey hair was cut short, almost like a man's, and her mouth turned down in a permanent expression of disapproval. A deep furrow was etched between the dark eyebrows. Antonia thought the woman could only be in her fifties, yet she presented herself as someone much older. Now Mrs Barton ushered them into a gloomy little sitting room, where she served them strong tea and gritty rock cakes she told them she had baked herself – probably not very recently, judging by their hardness.

'Librarian, are you?' interrogated Mrs. Barton.

'Well, yes. This is my first job since qualifying. I really like working back here. It's such a friendly place,' stammered Antonia nervously, finding the atmosphere anything but.

'Don't understand libraries,' rumbled Mrs. Barton. 'People too mean to buy books themselves, always wanting everything for free. Wouldn't want a library book in the house, meself, dirty things, don't know where they've been.'

Antonia was too startled at first to say anything. She did so want to come to the defence of her readers, none of them scroungers who wanted something for nothing, and certainly all of them perfectly clean! However, George caught her eye and gave her a warning look. It obviously was not worth arguing with his mother. Looking around furtively, Antonia saw no books in the room, from a library or otherwise, and precious little else. The dark furniture carried few ornaments, and strangest of all, no family photographs. Antonia had not had what some people insisted was a normal family life, although her mother had done her best to create one on her own, so she was particularly sensitive to these matters.

The afternoon went by slowly and with difficulty. Mrs Barton seemed to make a point of undermining whatever Antonia tried to say about anything at all, even her harmless comment about how pretty the flowers had been in the little town's park that summer. The council gardeners had gone to some trouble with some very attractive hanging baskets and with their pride and joy, a floral county coat of arms.

'Ridiculous waste of money!' snapped Mrs. Barton, and that was that.

George was unusually quiet, but behaved with his mother more as if he were a respectful nephew than the widow's only son.

'I trust you're keeping good health since I saw you a week ago,' he ventured.

'Very well, thank you, the doctors haven't managed to kill me yet,' she grumped in reply. 'You'll have to wait a bit longer for your inheritance!'

Antonia was relieved when finally George stood up and announced, 'It's time we were going, Mother.' She could not help but notice the momentary expression of relief on Mrs Barton's hard features. Life was so unfair, she thought. Here was a mother and son who plainly could not stand each other, but her own deeply loved and loving mother had been taken from her so soon.

George was first out of the door, and as soon as his back was turned, Mrs Barton grasped Antonia's arm and hissed: 'You don't really want my son, do you? He's a bad lot!' Antonia gaped at her, but there was no mistaking the look of fear on Mrs Barton's face. She glanced at George. He had turned round and was watching them.

'Well done,' he sighed, as the door slammed shut behind them. 'I really appreciate you making the effort with her. I suppose I should have warned you, but I was afraid you wouldn't come. I do everything to try to please her, but nothing seems to work. Thank you for your support, Antonia.'

She looked at him, and saw a man who was dejected and tired. She felt in that moment overwhelmingly sorry for him. She wanted to make up for Mrs Barton's sternness and coldness towards her only child. What on earth must life have been like for him as a little boy? 'Your mother must be a very unhappy person if she behaves as she does. Perhaps you should feel sorry for her.'

'Dear Antonia,' he laughed, 'always thinking the best of people. Even if you did get away to London for a bit, you have led a sheltered life.' He took hold of her hand firmly, and together they walked back towards the town. He was silent for a while, then suddenly asked, 'What did she say to you, there on the doorstep?' Antonia was naturally truthful, but some instinct told her not to tell him. 'Oh, something about you not being as rich as I thought you were.'

'Enough!' she told herself, sitting up in her bed high up in the attics of the Quattromani villa. 'I escaped from him, so why dwell on the past?' Antonia wriggled back under the sheet and fell into a doze.

She was wakened by a slight noise coming from the garden of the villa. In that soft, silent night, the sound carried crisp and clear. Then it came again, unmistakable now as the crunch of a footstep upon the gravel. Antonia caught her breath with fear, convinced she could hear her heart beating loudly in the silence. Who could it be, roaming around the villa at this time of night? Clutching her nightdress against her body and lifting her mobile from the bedside table, she moved swiftly in the direction of the window, checking the time. It was a little after two in the morning. Antonia was still a bit shaken from her dream, and all sorts of wild thoughts about George following her from England rushed up to scare her even more. But curiosity overcame her fear.

She realised that if she stood slightly to one side of the window, and far enough back, whoever this prowler was, he would not be able to see her. Once she had seen who it was, she could alert Luigi. The most likely explanation was that this person was after one of the countess's valuable thoroughbreds. Thank goodness for that bad dream. Usually Antonia slept soundly.

She tiptoed to the window, holding her breath with concentration, and looked down.

In the moonlight she saw him clearly. Lorenzo stood

looking toward the house, naked to the waist, his hands thrust into the pockets of the linen trousers that sat so easily on his hips, just exposing his navel. Antonia could not hold back a tiny gasp of wonder. He was the most beautiful sight she had ever seen or even imagined. The anger, the shock and the humiliation he had caused her the previous day were forgotten, and she admired him as she might admire a work of art. But this was no cold marble. This was a man. She longed to touch the tousled black hair, run her fingertips down the strong cords of his neck, across his taut stomach.

Don't go there! Lorenzo could not apparently see her, so with her face burning, she feasted her eyes upon him. *All right, where's the harm in looking?*

Lorenzo hardly moved. He merely tilted his head to one side, as though lost in thought. The image came back into her mind of his figure at the entrance to the tiny chapel, blocking her escape. But now she no longer thought of him with anger but with hopeless longing. Her head told her otherwise, but in her heart she knew she wanted him to kiss her, not in an entitled way, but with tenderness. A feeling she had never experienced before washed over her as she drank him in with her eyes. Certainly she knew she had never felt like this when she was with George, or with anyone before him. She felt a flush deepen down her neck. A delicious sensation crept through her body, a sensation of opening and softening, of wanting. Of demanding to be satisfied. She knew instinctively that the cry of her body could only be silenced by feeling the press of his weight against her. No one had never made her feel quite like this.

'I want you, Lorenzo,' she breathed, almost in spite of herself. Forgetting that she could be seen, she moved closer to the window. 'Oh, how I want you.'

Aware he was being watched, Lorenzo raised his head and looked straight up into Antonia's face. He could see her clearly in that silvery light, in her sleeveless white nightgown, with her chestnut curls tumbling about her bare shoulders. They gazed at each other for a few moments. Finally, he raised his hand for a moment in greeting before he turned on his heel and walked away into the shadows.

Chapter Four

Pull yourself together, you stupid, stupid girl! Her thumping heartbeat gradually went back to normal. *What on earth will he think now? You didn't want to encourage him, and now you've done just that!* She sank down on her bed, despairing. She was embarrassed, ashamed and more than a little frightened by the feelings the sight of Lorenzo's half-naked body had awoken in her. To send these feelings back to where they came from, if not kill them off altogether, Antonia forced herself to think of the beautiful Giselle. With deliberate ruthlessness she told herself that she could be no match for the elegant, accomplished Swiss girl. And they looked so good together.

How can you possibly think he'd be interested in you, when he's engaged to her? And all that stuff about other women wanting him for what they could get? That must be well up those any list of red flags. She could not, though, prevent the stab of pain in her heart that Lorenzo had gone from his night-time walk to lay that beautiful body of his alongside Giselle's. Antonia forced herself not to think about anything else they might be doing now. Her pride groaned at the nagging suspicion that all this was some elaborate practical joke at her expense. But she took comfort from the thought that Giselle would be away in a few days, and without his fiancée there to egg him on, there probably would not be any fun in teasing her anymore. Lorenzo's visit was unexpected and clearly not welcomed by his aunt, so perhaps Lorenzo would not linger much once he was on his own. And anyway, work was always a welcome refuge and would keep her out of his way. But, she asked herself, what on earth had he been doing out there below her window? She groaned inwardly. Had he already known where she slept? He certainly did now. Impossible man! Antonia wrung the cotton of her nightdress in her fists.

I don't even like the man. He's arrogant, overbearing, immoral and probably lazy. He doesn't appear to have a job, even. So why, oh why, should I want him so? Has his thoughtless kiss, a bit of fun and amusement for him no doubt, really put me so far into his hands? It had, she had to admit to herself. His beauty allowed him privileges denied to other men, and what was worse, he knew it. *There's only one way of salvaging the situation. He'd nothing to lose trying to kiss me – if that's all he was thinking of doing. But what about my peace of mind? After all the effort I went to when I split up from George... It's not like Lorenzo is going to leave that beautiful girl for me. That's an absurd idea. No, the only thing I can do is to ignore him, treat him with the distant politeness English people are supposed to be so good at.* Antonia could not help but laugh at that thought. *At least my pride will be intact that way, and with any luck he'll give up and leave me alone.* Having sorted things out as best she could in her own mind, Antonia slipped beneath the covers and fell asleep, fitfully aware of strange and disturbing dreams.

Stretched out on his bed, carefully not touching the sleeping Giselle, Lorenzo stared wide-awake at the ceiling. *La acia di un angelo* – the face of an angel – he kept repeating to himself. That was what he had seen framed in Antonia's window, a slim figure in a gauzy white shift, her hair tumbled about her shoulders like a dark halo. He was not going to have a restful night.

In spite of all her resolutions to be cool and distant, Antonia went down to breakfast the following morning with her heart thumping. *The worst of this will be over once I've seen him this morning,* she kept telling herself to steel her nerve. She saw the countess look searchingly at her as she hesitated at the door of the dining room. *I wish I could stop my hands shaking.* Neither Lorenzo nor Giselle had yet appeared, and Antonia did not know whether she should feel relief or annoyance that she still had to get this ordeal over with.

'Is something the matter?' asked the countess.

'No … not really. I didn't sleep that well.'

'Hmm … you'll no doubt tell me what it is in time. I'd be very surprised if that ne'er do well of a nephew of mine and that silly woman haven't got something to do with it.'

Antonia felt herself flush and was glad that the countess tactfully looked away, pouring herself more coffee. 'My dead brother was a weak, spoiled man, Antonia. Even when we were children I was always the stronger willed of the two of us. You're smiling! That's better!'

'I was just imaging you as a little girl.'

'I was bossy even then. And now I've had more than eighty years of practice, so I'm even worse! I am afraid that Lorenzo may have inherited the faults of his father, though I must say the boy does seem to have brains. A dangerous combination. And then you come here, a capable, hard-working girl, attempting to make your way in the world, on your own too, and apparently making a success of it. Don't let anyone spoil that, my dear.'

'I won't.'

'That's the spirit. Now come and sit by me, my dear,' she said, indicating the nearest chair. 'You look a little tired. I'm sure I have been working you too hard.'

'Oh, but I love our work!' Antonia hastened to reassure her.

'I know you do, I know,' the countess replied warmly.

'That shows through in everything you do. We have a large task, though, a responsibility to posterity as well as to our own dear Gianluca.'

Antonia laughed. 'I feel like I know him personally by now!'

'That's good. It'll help you stay enthusiastic,' continued the old lady. 'We owe Gianluca that. Now, he was an explorer, an adventurer. It's only fair we stay true to his memory and do a bit of exploring ourselves. This is Tuscany, the most beautiful landscape in the most beautiful country in the world – you'll forgive me if I'm biased, I'm sure. You ought to see it for yourself, so I suggest a little jaunt today. Besides,' and here she leaned forward conspiratorially and patted Antonia's hand as her voice dropped to a whisper, 'you would do me a great favour. I don't think I wish to spend any more of my valuable time with that blackguard of a nephew and that dashed adventuress of his.'

Antonia smiled at the old lady's slightly quaint, old-fashioned English, but her eyes prickled with tears of gratitude. *She can't possibly know everything that has happened, but she's sensed something's wrong and has come up with a perfect alternative to a day I was dreading.* Instinctively Antonia felt in that moment that before long she would be able to confide in the countess, and that her advice and counsel could be trusted completely. A calmness, a sense of belonging washed over her. She began at last to feel at home, a valued confidante, more than an employee.

Just then she heard the soft tread of the panther as he stalked across the marble floor of the hall and into the dining room, but this time she knew that she, his prey, was safe from his claws. In the sobering light of day all Lorenzo did was to wish her a polite good morning, much to her relief.

'And what about our other visitor?' grated out Lorenzo's aunt. He shrugged briefly.

'She must still be asleep,' he murmured, as he drew back a chair and sat further down the table, pulling the jug of fresh coffee towards him.

What an odd thing to say. A feeble hope stirred in Antonia's heart. He had not, apparently, taken advantage of what she thought of as the sweetest privilege allowed to established lovers, to watch the beloved awaken. With his next words to his aunt, Lorenzo confirmed this.

'I went up to the olive groves this morning. I took the mare up. I hope that was all right. This year's is going to be a good crop, but some of the trees will need replacing next season.'

The countess looked surprised. 'I didn't know you took such an interest. You didn't always. And that's fine about the horse, she needs to get used to as many different riders as possible.'

Lorenzo went on, with growing enthusiasm. 'And some of the terraces need repair. This year's heavy rain has dislodged even some of the larger stones. Once Giselle's away I could go up with Alessio to repair them.'

Antonia was pleased to see the countess smile.

'Alessio has been with the estate longer than anyone

else,' said the old lady, 'and he's always taken personal responsibility for the olive groves, but he knows and I know that he's getting a little too old to cope with the work. But no one knows these hills the way he does. As a child he used to run messages for the partisans fighting the blackshirts and Nazis, from their hideouts up there. To relieve him of his duties even on the lower slopes would be to deprive him of his birthright. So I think Alessio would really appreciate working with you on the terraces. Be sure and do exactly what he tells you. He can't manage all the physical work anymore, but there is nothing wrong with his expertise.'

Lorenzo had said *once Giselle's away*. Antonia felt her courage ebb. So he really did intend to stay on a while. What then? Her musings were interrupted by the arrival of Giselle herself. She strolled into the room in an exquisite dark blue silk wrap, not having bothered to dress, her hair lying in deliberate disorder about her shoulders. The shimmering material could not hope to hide the free movement of her full breasts, the proud points of her nipples. She ignored the other two women in the room, wrapping her arms instead around Lorenzo's shoulders so that the back of his head nestled between those breasts.

'Darling, you are so splendid,' she purred.

The countess frowned deeply, but merely shook out her linen napkin vigorously, while Antonia fixed her eyes on her plate, dreading seeing what Lorenzo's reaction might be to Giselle's caresses. But her resolve to maintain her polite reserve was actually strengthened by Giselle's blatant possession of him. He was forbidden territory, the Swiss girl made that perfectly clear, and this made things easier for her. Antonia looked up to see Lorenzo reach up to pat Giselle's hands, as if to reassure her, but this obvious gesture could not disguise the slight, almost imperceptible movement of his shoulders, as if he wanted to dislodge the fawning girl.

Breakfast was the one meal of the day at which Luigi was not in attendance, but what had promised to be a normal, happy, domestic occasion had altered with Giselle's appearance on the scene. For a brief moment Antonia had seen aunt and nephew almost on good terms. Instead the countess now finished eating in stony silence. She did not get up to leave even when she had finished her breakfast, and Antonia suddenly realised that her employer was discreetly waiting for her to finish too. The old lady had the tact and delicacy not to leave her alone with the couple who had sneered at her from the moment they arrived.

The countess stepped nimbly up the steep, cobble-stoned path that led to the little ruined tower. She had her stick for support, but even though she was in her eighties, Laura Quattromani was a fit, spry woman. Antonia trotted along behind her, and both were slightly out of breath by the time they reached the stone bench at the base of the tower. The bench was a splendid vantage point from which to see over the valley. They looked down on a lush landscape of vineyards and clusters of red-tiled roofs of farm buildings.

A church bell was ringing in an ancient stone belfry, and its sound echoed across to them.

'This little ruin is known as Dante's tower,' the old lady informed Antonia. 'It is said that this is where the poet found sanctuary when he was first expelled from Florence. Our regional capital was then a powerful and independent city state, and it stayed that way by virtue of a ruthless intolerance of political opposition. Our poor poet backed the wrong side, and was sent into exile. This was far enough to satisfy his persecutors, but it didn't stop him from writing.' This was said with some relish, and as the countess continued, Antonia realised why.

'I used to come here often when I was very small, wondering what it must feel like to be banished from home. I didn't think even then, although Mussolini was already in power, that it would happen to me too. Father sent Mother and me away to friends in England before anything could happen to any of us, but self-imposed exile is exile just the same. History has this habit of repeating itself,' she added with a wry smile.

'Didn't your brothers and sisters go too?' queried Antonia, wondering just how Lorenzo fitted into all this. The countess's expression darkened.

'I only had one brother, older than me, and he stayed behind. A weak-willed, unprincipled young man he was, obsessed with his good looks.' She laughed, a bitter and joyless sound. 'He probably thought that absurd fascist uniform suited him. Anyway, he was making quite a career with the regime. It nearly broke my father's heart. When we came back to Italy after the liberation my father signed away the Gavedo estates, fifty miles north, to my brother, his only son, on condition he never had to see or hear from him again. He wouldn't have cut him off without a penny, you see, because my father had a great sense of responsibility, and because Italian law does not permit complete disinheritance, but he never wanted to be reminded of him and what he saw as his betrayal. So the larger part of the Quattromani inheritance came to me, which was unusual for a girl, but Father had always known I would look after it well.'

The old lady's voice quavered and went silent, and Antonia saw with concern and anxiety that Laura Quattromani's eyes were filled with the tears of a sorrow decades old.

The countess dashed them away impatiently with the back of her hand and her voice recovered its strength as she said roughly, 'Well, what use is it to rake over the past? The fascists did many terrible things. My nephew is the son of a fascist – he has my brother's face. Some of his character, too. My brother was well into middle-age when he seduced Lorenzo's mother; she was thirty years younger. The wolf changes his pelt but not his vices. What is it you say in English?'

'The leopard doesn't change his spots.'

'That's right. I'm getting forgetful.'

Antonia trembled. There was an unmistakable warning

in the old lady's words. She did not know what words to use to respond to this story, so instead she simply reached for the countess's hand. The countess's reaction was to take Antonia's and to hold it tightly between both her own. No wonder, thought Antonia, that Lorenzo's presence was so distasteful to his aunt. Antonia was in turmoil, torn between her compassion for the countess and the growing feelings she had for Lorenzo, feelings that she knew she could not deny. *I would dearly love to tell her how I feel, but how can I?* Lorenzo had arrived in Antonia's life with all the shattering impact of a thunderbolt. She realised the situation was hopeless, but longed for someone to confide in. Now she knew that someone could not be the countess.

Antonia saw less and less of Lorenzo. He was as good as his word to his aunt, almost as if he had something to prove. She saw that he spent his time working on the estates, clearly learning Alessio's craft, just as his ancestors' farmworkers had for centuries. Lorenzo put aside his elegant designer linen suits and shirts for serviceable old cotton clothes and boots that protected his ankles from snakes. Were it not for his superior height and his unmistakably aristocratic bone structure, he could have passed for an estate servant, used all his life to working outdoors. The warm, deep tan, nurtured on a private beach on the Riviera, gradually gave way to the tough, weather-beaten look of the countryman. His cared-for hands had become calloused, broader somehow and visibly stronger. Above all, the languid look of boredom in the slate-grey eyes had been replaced by a look of purpose and with it peace and tranquillity. Heavy manual work under the hot July sun obviously suited him, body and soul.

Even the atmosphere between him and his aunt seemed to have relaxed. Antonia saw him only at mealtimes, or occasionally from a distance, exercising the horses in the paddock with the practised air of someone who had been in the saddle as soon as he could walk. He was now always courteous to her, while to his aunt he was voluble about his work on improving the estate. Although Antonia was fast picking up colloquial Italian from the other estate employees, the countess made it a point of good manners towards her that all these conversations at mealtimes should be in English. Antonia too could not fail to be impressed by Lorenzo's activity. She really did not know what to make of him. Who, she wondered, was the real Lorenzo Quattromani?

At least there were no surprises as far as Giselle Landsdorf was concerned. Lorenzo's energy contrasted with her almost complete inertia. For the remainder of her short stay she simply sunbathed. Seemingly the only time she moved was when she snapped her fingers at Luigi or Elena to bring her out another drink – she had never again tried to treat Antonia as a servant. One day she had roared off to the seaside in the silver Mercedes, but not until after she had had an argument with Lorenzo in front of the villa that Antonia could not fail to hear, even high up in her rooms. At first she tried hard not to listen, but temptation got the better of her. She could not understand all that was being shouted, but made out the gist of the argument.

'What sort of a man are you, anyway? I'm going to be away shortly for a whole month and you don't even want to be with me!' screamed Giselle.

'I've told you already, this estate needs a lot of attention. Aunt can't manage to oversee everything now, and Alessio can teach me so much. How can I make you understand that?' retorted Lorenzo.

'You and your precious aunt. She's not going to leave you anything, lover. Why do you bother? And you'll turn into a peasant yourself, the time you spend with that old fool of a labourer. It's time he was in an old people's home!' she shot back.

'Strange as it may seem, Giselle, I'm not doing this for my aunt because I expect anything from her. I'm looking for no more than her respect! And what gives you the right to talk about Alessio like that? I don't care if I do turn into a peasant. I'd rather be a peasant than one of those idle rich types you have as clients!' Lorenzo's voice was raised, but he kept a level, controlled tone. Antonia could not miss the anger that simmered underneath.

'Well, you have changed your tune, haven't you?' came Giselle's sneering response. 'You'll tell me next how much you respect that librarian your aunt has slaving for her. Perhaps she's your ideal woman. You probably deserve each other, so self-righteous, so boring!'

Lorenzo's answer was lost in the roar of the powerful engine and the slam of the car door. The Mercedes sped off towards the airport. Although she had done nothing wrong, Antonia was left with a feeling of terrible guilt. Giselle's words had touched a raw nerve. Lorenzo's ideal woman? If only!

When Giselle finally left for New York, Louis Vuitton suitcases piled high inside the Mercedes, she did not even honour Antonia and the countess with so much as a cursory wave, just an unsmiling look from behind dark glasses. Lorenzo drove her away dressed again as Antonia had seen him the first time they'd met, with casual, understated elegance. Giselle must have told him she didn't want to be taken anywhere by anyone looking like a farm labourer.

'Well! Thank goodness for small mercies!' exclaimed the countess, stomping back into the villa. 'I'm even beginning to think that there's a shadow of a good side to my nephew. Old Alessio seems very impressed with the work he's doing, but when will he change his taste in women? That one is a real bloodsucker!'

'He does seem to have taken on all that work with a lot of enthusiasm,' ventured Antonia tentatively. After all, she thought, he did come here for a holiday. If he really was trying to convince his aunt that he was more than just his father's son, then he was not sparing any effort. Antonia had it on the tip of her tongue to tell the countess about what she had overheard, about how Lorenzo simply wanted his aunt's respect, but she was ashamed to admit that she had been listening, and of what Giselle had said about her.

The countess laughed in reply. 'I should think he's been learning from your good example, my dear. You don't loll around on the terrace all day drinking Campari. You take work seriously. The archive is coming along splendidly. I shall die content!' she shouted melodramatically, waving her stick in the air.

'Oh, don't talk like that,' cried Antonia, only half-pretending to be shocked. The two women went into what they now described as their inner sanctum, the library, and that morning the work seemed to go better than ever, the bits of the jigsaw slotting into place. Passages of manuscript that had looked indecipherable the day before suddenly looked crystal clear on the yellowed pages. *Yes, this is an exceptionally good day, and*, as Antonia thought a little guiltily, *Giselle's departure has to have something to do with it.* But if she were honest with herself, the thought of lolling around on the terrace drinking Campari did have some appeal. Just once in a while it would be nice to be spoiled a bit too.

Antonia and the countess took lunch alone but for the presence of Luigi, as Lorenzo had not yet returned from the airport. Afterwards, Antonia took her customary walk. She now felt so in command of herself that she resolved on taking the path that she had chosen that fateful day when Lorenzo had pushed her against the wall of the deserted chapel. She wanted to explore the direction he had taken after she had thrust him away from her. She would be past the chapel in seconds, she told herself, and then she would not need to dwell on what had happened there any longer.

As she started her ascent to the little chapel, she became gradually aware of a sweet, pervasive scent in the warm air, the scent of familiar flowers. The slightest trace of a faintly remembered scent could always recreate the emotions of a moment in the past for her far more vividly than any music or picture, and with her heart beating faster, she recognised the scent of white lilies, the aroma of the flowers she had stooped to smell that day when Lorenzo had crept up on her unawares. It grew stronger, almost overpoweringly so as she climbed on. She could not help but look upwards as the little chapel came into view on the summit, and gasped at the sight. The normally dark interior of the tiny building shimmered ivory and green in the afternoon light. It was full of lilies, standing all around the walls, strewn across the floor, and framing the little plaque of the Virgin Mary and the baby Jesus. Antonia gazed at them, open-mouthed. This could surely only be Lorenzo's doing. What kind of a man really was he? Could it be his way of saying sorry?

Chapter Five

Antonia descended slowly from the chapel, having decided after the surprise of finding all those flowers to explore the path beyond it another day. The countess would be finishing her siesta soon, so she decided to go straight to the library and meet her there. Today, when Antonia entered the room, the library appeared empty, although the countess could not be far away. Her reading glasses were there, perched on a pile of papers.

Antonia had started setting up her laptop, getting ready for work, when she was startled by a groan so faint she thought she must have imagined it. Then she heard it again, barely louder than a whisper. She jumped to her feet, her heart thumping, and looked anxiously up and down the room. The library had an old-fashioned gallery to make best use of the height of the walls, reached by a spiral staircase. It was on this gallery that Antonia caught sight of the crumpled figure of the countess, lying beside an upturned set of library steps. Antonia clattered up the cast-iron staircase as fast as her legs could carry her.

The countess was grey with shock and pain, but her face flooded with obvious relief when she saw Antonia. One side of her face was bruised and bleeding slightly where she had caught it against the library steps in her fall, but from her pale lips came only the words 'My leg, I've hurt my leg!' As Antonia saw, one leg was indeed twisted up under her at a strange angle.

'Don't move, whatever you do,' warned Antonia urgently, worried that the old lady might shift a broken bone and do even more damage. 'I'll get help!' Laura Quattromani nodded slightly, winced with the pain, and then her head relaxed. She had fainted. There was no time to be lost. Antonia hurtled back down the spiral staircase, risking broken bones herself, and out of the library. 'Ambulanza! Ambulanza!' she shouted out into the hall. She had not even realised that she knew the Italian for ambulance, but the word came out when she needed it. Without thinking even about how she was going to communicate, she picked up the telephone that looked oddly out of place on an antique marble-topped table, and in seconds she was through to the emergency services. A calm and unflustered voice told her to go back to the countess, keep her warm, put a cushion under her head if she was already moving it about of her own accord, but otherwise not to move her. It was only later that Antonia realised she had carried on the entire conversation in competent Italian, without even noticing that was what she was doing.

Luigi by now had rushed into the hall, having heard her shouts, and had caught the end of her conversation. 'What has happened, Signorina? Where is *la contessa*?' he gasped out, a little short of breath.

'She's had a fall in the library and hurt herself,' answered Antonia, surprised at the calmness of her own voice. 'She needs a blanket and a cushion. The ambulance is on its way.'

The reliable Luigi melted away and within a couple of minutes reappeared in the library with the necessary articles. Antonia had returned to the countess's side, and was kneeling beside her, stroking her hands and murmuring reassuring words. The old lady's eyes flickered open and shut, but their expression was one of trust and relief. She was lying still and calm now, and as she was able to move her head.

Antonia eased the cushion underneath it and tucked the blanket around her. 'I'll go and wait for the ambulance team, tell them where to go,' said Luigi. 'And I'll send for the young master.'

The young master! Antonia had clean forgotten him in this crisis. But of course, Luigi was right. It looked as if the countess could be away from the villa for some while, unless she was lucky and there was not too much damage done. Her nephew, labouring up on the hillside with Alessio, was her nearest relative and would for the time being be master of this place. A man who had gazed up at Antonia's window on a moonlit night. A man who filled a ruined little chapel with lilies as if asking forgiveness …

The wail of a siren broke into Antonia's thoughts. The ambulance was already on the road coming up to the estate, and seconds later, Luigi was explaining matters rapidly to the two paramedics who were carrying a stretcher into the house. Antonia stood aside as they began the delicate task of ascertaining the extent of Laura Quattromani's injuries and preparing her to be lifted onto their stretcher. They were efficient, rapid but at the same time unrushed and extremely gentle in their work. But despite all their care, the agonising sound of bone grinding on bone was inevitable as they started to lift their patient. As brave as any soldier, the old lady let out only the smallest moan and gritted her teeth. Getting her down the spiral staircase was going to be awkward, so they tied straps around her body and let her down almost vertically. When the little group reached the ground, there was a collective sigh of relief and compliments to the paramedics from Luigi, his face tight with worry.

Antonia hung back as the two professionals loaded their patient into the ambulance, anxious not to get in the way, until one of them gestured to her to climb in too.

'The lady has had a great shock. It is better that you stay with her, *signorina*,' one explained.

As the ambulance began its journey to the hospital, the countess opened her eyes.

'Oh my dear, I do appreciate your being here,' faltered the old lady, a spot of colour starting to come into the grey cheeks now that the first shock was over and she knew that everything was under control.

'Hush, just rest,' Antonia soothed her. 'We'll be at the hospital soon.'

'I'm so sorry. What a silly impatient old woman I am. I should have waited for you. The trouble is I just don't appreciate how old I am!' continued the countess in a sorry tone, but with just a hint of defiance nevertheless. Antonia knew then that if the countess had anything to do with it, hers was going to be a quick recovery. She might be nearly eighty, but she was still a fighter, strong and determined. Antonia could not help feeling just a tiny bit sorry for the doctors who were going to be dealing with her. Advice to lie down and rest would not be accepted willingly.

They reached the hospital in the market town within twenty minutes, and as they were expecting her, the countess was seen immediately. Antonia sat out in the corridor while the old lady was examined. After what seemed an age, a white-coated doctor came out to speak to her. Antonia was reassured by his kind face, his patient manner and the grey hair that indicated experience.

'Signorina Gray? Thank you for waiting. As is usual on these occasions, there is good news and bad news, but I'm happy to say that this time it's mainly good. The lady hit her head slightly as she fell, but fortunately it was only a superficial blow. She is only slightly concussed. What is more serious is that she has smashed her hip, and we really have no option but to replace it. So she will be here for a little while yet, but at the end of it all she will actually be in better shape than if she had never had the accident at all. She is sedated now, to kill the pain, and we'll operate tomorrow morning. Can you come to see her again tomorrow evening? I am sure she would appreciate that very much, as she keeps asking for you, and so,' he added smiling, 'would we. I think she'll be a very restless patient. It will not be easy for her to obey my instructions.'

'Of course, I'll visit her every day. I'll be back tomorrow with some of her things.'

'A good idea.' The doctor patted her hand. 'Now we should get you back home. Can I call you a taxi?'

'That won't be necessary, thank you, *dottore*,' a man's voice cut in from behind them. It was an oddly cultured voice considering its owner's rough workman's clothing. There was nothing else that was rough about the man, however. Lorenzo had come to the hospital as soon as he had heard, without bothering to change. Now he stretched out a hand to Antonia, indicating to her to rise.

'Let me take you home, Antonia,' he said gently, and with his hand proprietorially on her elbow, Lorenzo guided her out of the hospital and towards the Mercedes parked under the trees. He opened the passenger door for her, making sure that she was settled comfortably in her seat before he closed it.

He did not speak for some minutes after they drove off.

Antonia watched him shyly out of the corner of her eye. This was the first time they had been in such close proximity to each other since their encounter in the chapel. His first words surprised her, although by now she was learning to expect surprises from this man.

'You won't go away, will you?'

'Go away? What do you mean, back to England?' she asked.

'Yes. My aunt has come to rely on you, anyone can see that. She's not such an easy person to get on with, a demanding person, a perfectionist. She has high standards. But she has certainly taken to you. You've earned her respect.' He said these last words with just a tinge of bitterness.

'Of course I'm not going away,' replied Antonia, 'I've got a job to do. I'm really a bit of a perfectionist myself. And besides, I've got nowhere to go.'

He glanced at her in surprise. 'Nowhere to go? What about your family? Your home?'

'I gave up my home and my job to come here. My mother is dead and my father is goodness knows where. He's been as good as dead for an awful lot longer than Mother.'

'Poor girl,' he murmured sympathetically. 'But you don't behave like a poor girl. Quite a survivor. It was brave of you to come all this way. And then you get taken advantage of.'

She felt the heat in her face, a conflict of emotions coursing through her. His words reminded her so much of the kind things George had said to her, before she discovered his true character. It was true, he *had* tried to take advantage of her trusting nature for his own purposes, and had almost succeeded. Antonia was determined not to fall into the same trap again. Lorenzo, she felt sure, was also setting a trap for her, with the difference that this time she longed above all to fall into it. She wanted this man in a way she had never wanted anyone. She'd never known she could want anyone so much. And now she was so close to him. For a crazy moment she imagined burying her head in his neck, drinking in the smell of him, and her hands itched to stroke his thick black wavy hair, to pull his head towards her.

'That's something we have in common – being a survivor, I mean,' he remarked, breaking the silence that had again settled between them. Antonia was startled. Why on earth was this handsome, rich, aristocratic but deeply unsettled and unsettling man describing himself as a survivor? What could he know about what it was like to literally have no place to go to, no place of his own? As if reading her thoughts, he explained himself.

'My mother and father died in a plane crash while I was away at school. But even when I was at home during the school holidays I never really seemed to get to know them. Another odd thing is that they never married – part of his fecklessness, really, though my father recognised me as his and I have his name. That's why I have no title. That's why my aunt is the countess, rather than me being a count. I never will be, either, unless she decides to formally recognise me as her heir. The nearest I got to a mother was really my dear Irish nanny. So you see, I too know the meaning of loneliness.'

'How can you?' Antonia finally burst out. 'You have everything you could possibly want, and Giselle too.' At the same time she was shocked at the idea of two wealthy parents who had practically given up responsibility for bringing up their own child to others.

'Antonia, how little you know,' he sighed. 'Please let me talk to you. That's all I want. I won't push myself at you again, I promise. There's just you and me now. My aunt's in hospital, Giselle's doing whatever it is she wants to do. I'm not in love with her, you know, and I'm pretty convinced she's not in love with me. I suppose I'm useful to her, and that we look good together, whatever that means. That's all. The rest is really just habit now.'

'Why are you telling me all this?' asked Antonia tremulously.

'Because I think you've got the wrong idea about me. That's my own fault, of course. I was so rude to you when I first met you. Forgive me,' he pleaded softly, unexpectedly.

Antonia did not know what to say. All she could manage was a rather stiff, 'Don't mention it.' What was she to think? The man changed like a weather-vane. He laughed briefly before replying.

'How English you are, you and your *don't mention it*. I wonder if I'll ever know what you are really thinking.' *Point taken*, thought Antonia. By now they were back at the villa and the Mercedes came to a halt.

'Thank you for bringing me back,' she said breathlessly, fumbling for the door handle. He leaned across her to help, so close that she felt his breath on her cheek and an electric tingling as for a moment his hair brushed her skin. She was conscious of his warmth, the musky male smell of him, the tensed muscles of his forearm, and his broad, strong hand almost but not quite touching her. Then the door opened, and he drew back. Antonia slipped out and dashed towards the entrance.

'Antonia! Wait a minute!' he called. She halted and turned round and watched him climb out of the car. 'Let me say just one more thing,' he said, walking towards her. He placed his hands gently on her shoulders and looked into her upturned face.

'You're beautiful, lonely girl, believe me. Probably you don't know it, and that makes you even more attractive, but it's true.'

'Oh please!' muttered Antonia in confusion, and wriggled out of his grasp. As she ran in through the door she heard him call out, 'Don't mention it!'

Without stopping or looking once over her shoulder, she rushed straight up to her rooms. Once inside, she leaned a moment against the back of the door, panting more from excitement at Lorenzo's electric touch and his words than because she had taken the steps two at a time. Then she caught sight of her own image reflected in the mirror at the other side of the room. She approached it carefully, warily, then stood for some minutes wonderingly observing herself. It was true what he had said. For the first time in her life Antonia realised that she could be beautiful, that she was beautiful. The Italian sun, the clean air of these mountains and fields, and above all, the words of that man she had tried to keep away from had made this change in her. She saw now what he saw, as though for the first time in her life, the rich abandon of her chestnut hair, the warmth of her pale gold tan suffused with a blush that made her whole face glow with life, the deepening blue of her eyes and the shell pink of her softly opened mouth. There was nothing sophisticated about her beauty. She had nothing of the hard, enamelled perfection of Giselle. Her loveliness lay instead in her naturalness, her freshness, her innocence – an English rose. Her blush deepened as for a moment she imagined her own face upon a lace pillow, her bright hair strewn about, his face dark with passion above hers. With a cry she flung herself on her bed.

'I mustn't, I can't – oh, why do I never learn?'

Lorenzo's behaviour towards Antonia was now as courteous as it had once been overbearing. She could not help but wonder if it was partly his aristocratic inheritance that made him divide females into servants and the served. Antonia had refused to let him treat her as a servant, and as a result he had become respectful towards her.

They took their meals together in the great dining room, emptier than ever now that the commanding presence of the countess was absent from the head of the table. One lunch time he said to her, only half in jest, 'You know, we two eating here could be any old married couple.'

'H-how do you mean?' stammered Antonia, just managing not to drop her fork.

'Well, maybe not any old married couple. I mean a Quattromani marriage, the kind I know best. Just think of how this family became powerful through medieval times. It wasn't only military might, although that had a lot to do with it. There were all those rich, dynastic marriages, nothing to do with love, all to do with adding to the estates. There must have been so much misery in those liaisons. As you know, that's one reason why Gianluca Quattromani became such a traveller. Anything but the domestic ordeal of a loveless marriage. Once his son was born he and his wife lived apart, not impossible in a place this size. It is said that there were times in the history of this family when all the Quattromani children bore a startling resemblance to the head ostler, and at other times many children born in the village looked more like the count of that time than like their mothers' husbands. Every human being needs love and comfort,' he added with some sincerity, 'and why not? As long as appearances were kept up, then everyone was happy. Meeting at mealtimes, going to church together.'

'Are you suggesting that we should go to church?' asked

Antonia, laughing.

'Oh no,' he responded, in a mock-serious tone. 'People might talk. Where would the comfort and love be in that?' Antonia's throat tightened, and she pretended to concentrate on her food.

'I'm sorry, I didn't mean to embarrass you,' he added hastily. 'Listen, why don't I take you up to Gavedo one of these days? I'd like to show you something of the other Quattromani lands, let you see how the black sheep lives.' He gave a short, low laugh, like the villain's laugh in a melodrama.

'Well, yes, thank you for asking me. I should like that very much,' she answered. 'Gianluca wrote about the castle at Gavedo in a number of his letters, and I think it would really help my work if I could see it and not just imagine it.'

'I'm afraid old Gianluca wouldn't like to see it so much now. The castle suffered a lot during the war, and nothing has been done to it since then except shore it up against further collapse. It's really a magnificent ruin. The oldest parts of it, which are actually the sturdiest, are now used as barns. But I'm glad you'd like to see it. It's a dream of mine, you see,' and his voice lowered, 'to restore Gavedo to its former glory. It needs to be put to some good use though, and I can't think what. I tried to interest my aunt in it, but she wants nothing to do with that part of Quattromani territory. It's not surprising, really.'

'Because of her brother?' she enquired softly.

'Ah, so you know about him? My aunt really does trust you. She never talks about that time, normally, although all the older people connected with the estates of course know all about it. There were so many divisions here, not just in this family. Yes, let me take you to Gavedo. But it might be wisest not to say anything to my aunt about it.'

Antonia frowned. 'No, Lorenzo, not in that case. I wouldn't want to go behind her back and betray her trust, especially now she's confined to a hospital ward.'

He leaned forward.

'I know, Antonia, and I'm glad you said that, it's worthy of you. But I would so like to show you something of mine. I would take my aunt there if she'd let me, I'd try to show her that I'm more than her brother's son.' He reached for her hand and held it tightly, urgently in both his own. They were warm, dry, strong hands, roughened by the work he had been doing to reconstruct the stone terraces.

Antonia was torn between her loyalty to the countess, Lorenzo's obvious sincerity, and, she had to admit to herself, the opportunity to spend all that time alone in his company. *So much for my good intentions.* Her head told her no, but her heart told her that she never wanted him to take his hands away. Eventually she said, 'I would love to come with you. But I must tell the countess first. Tonight, during visiting hours. She's paying me for my time, it's the least I can do.'

'Thank you, my dear Antonina,' he exclaimed, using a

charming diminutive of her name that Antonia had never heard before. 'If she doesn't mind, we'll go tomorrow after an early breakfast. It's not that far, only about thirty of your English miles, though the road winds about a bit. That's settled then, but for today, back to work!' He grasped an imaginary spade and with a flourish pretended to dig.

Laura Quattromani was sitting up looking dangerously bored when Antonia came into the ward. The hip replacement operation had gone smoothly, but now the real challenge was how to prevent the patient from doing too much too soon. She pounced hungrily on everything Antonia had to say about her progress with the archive. But partway through her account, Laura interrupted Antonia. 'It's the highpoint of my day, listening to you,' she said, 'but something is bothering you. Out with it!'

'You know how Gavedo keeps coming up in the papers …'

'Yes, you can go!'

'Pardon?'

'My nephew has asked you if you want to see the place. Why else is the boy skulking about outside and not coming in to see me? Go, Antonia, but just don't tell me about your visit. I've not seen it for years, and it has bad memories for me … All right, you can tell me, not about the castle, but about what Lorenzo has done with the land. No harm in that. It looks as though he might make something out of himself at last. Nothing like doing a hand's turn to build character. You're good for him too. I can't pretend I haven't noticed. If that poisonous woman stays away long enough then who knows ...'

Antonia remembered an expression of her mother's, *I just didn't know where to put my face.* She found she could look anywhere but at the countess.

'Go and get that boy in here!' said Laura. 'I'll remind him he needs to drive carefully.'

The following morning brought with it another blaze of sunshine. Because it was a day out, Antonia decided to indulge herself, so she selected her favourite frock from her meagre wardrobe. It was a dress she had made herself, of roughly woven turquoise linen that didn't crease the way finer weaves did, with mother of pearl buttons down the front. The colour added lustre to her eyes, and its princess seams accentuated her neat curves and firm, high breasts. Antonia was never in the habit of wearing much makeup and today all that was needed with her lightly tanned, healthy complexion was a stroke of mascara and a touch of pearly lipstick. She decided against a scrunchie, letting her hair flow to her shoulders. A pair of light, strappy sandals completed the look.

However, her effect on Lorenzo was electrifying. As she came into the dining room his eyes widened a moment as he looked her up and down two or three times until his gaze flickered over the fullness of her breasts. Antonia panicked for a moment, wondering if she had been wise, and wishing she had stuck to a less feminine tee-shirt and cropped trousers. Was the predatory Lorenzo back, the Lorenzo who had followed her to the little chapel? Was the kind and considerate Lorenzo she had seen since his aunt's accident an act he could not keep up? Yet the less cautious part of her brain, the one that was unfurling like a flower in the warmth and beauty of Italy, told her that she enjoyed the effect she had on him, loved the blatant desire in his look. These contradictory thoughts rushed through Antonia's head, but just as quickly Lorenzo seemed to recover himself. He scraped back his chair and came towards her with a friendly smile.

'Antonia,' he said, taking her hands and looking at her at arm's length, his head tilted slightly as he appraised her. 'You look more lovely than ever, a Botticelli Primavera, or perhaps a Venus.'

Antonia felt herself flush at the comparison with these famous Renaissance paintings, the second of which was of a naked woman shielded only by her long hair. 'Thank you,' she managed to force out. After all, he had paid her a compliment.

They set off for Gavedo soon after eight, heading up through the foothills of the Apuan Alps. The big car purred effortlessly through tiny villages of rough stone houses with red-tiled roofs. The sound of church bells in high pink belfries resounded across the valleys. Herds of sheep and goats, each animal with an insistent, clanking little bell around its neck, slowed their journey. Outside a little bar old men sat in the morning sun, all of them wearing hats, all of them with strong cups of fresh coffee before them, while the plump landlady stood filling the doorway, hands on hips and pretending to scold them. On lichened walls cats lay lazily washing their faces, and geraniums spilled over from terrace gardens and up and down stone steps. This really is paradise. Even the most modest little houses were maintained with pride and care, the paths before them swept clean, pristine white lacework curtains at the windows. Every now and then they passed a ruined castle on a wooded hilltop. It seemed that most of these, according to Lorenzo, had belonged to some branch of the Quattromani family in times gone by. Others had been the property of rival families who had foolishly taken on the Quattromani might and had lost. Some of these little fortresses had been converted into homes for several families and had flowers hanging in baskets from windows where once defending archers had taken aim, or had washing hanging out to dry in courtyards which had once resounded to the clank of armour and medieval weaponry.

'It's so beautiful here,' Antonia breathed in wonderment.

'Yes,' he answered. 'When Dante wrote his Paradise he must surely have been thinking of his own Tuscany. In some ways little has changed since his day.'

The car climbed higher into the mountains, and the air

became even purer and clearer. The road wound more and more, for there was nothing that civil engineering could do here to challenge the grand architecture of nature. Tiny churches, hilltop sanctuaries, clung to outcrops of rock. The bare, craggy peaks of some of the highest mountains still carried streaks of snow, in contrast to the green richness of the valleys far below. At times, the hillside fell dizzyingly away below the road, giving the impression that it hung in the air. At other times the car hugged closely to a rock-face cutting. This was certainly not a road to travel in darkness, thought Antonia with a frisson of fear. Lorenzo, fortunately, was a confident but calm driver, and she felt safe in his company. Antonia shuddered at the thought of what Giselle would have been like on this road, judging by her driving that day she and Lorenzo had argued and she had screeched off alone at top speed to the seaside. Lorenzo noticed her slight movement and asked her with surprised concern, 'Are you cold? The air is much fresher up here.'

'Oh no, not at all. It's this landscape, it takes my breath away.'

'We'll start the descent towards Gavedo very soon,' he said. 'It won't be long now.'

Sure enough, before too long the car started on a steep descent into a lush valley with a lazy river at its heart, gurgling and bubbling over great rocks that had long ago rolled down the mountains and come to rest in the water. Presently Lorenzo took a left turn onto a bumpy road leading into the heart of a wood, and this road began to climb again gently. Antonia had by now lost all sense of direction, between the winding of the road and the peaks and valleys. Suddenly the woods cleared and they were passing through a straggling little hamlet. Unlike most villages in the area, this one appeared not to have a church of its own, until all of a sudden Antonia caught sight of one, a short distance away from the houses, with a little graveyard huddled around it. She saw to her surprise that the church was abandoned and stood roofless to the sky. She glanced at Lorenzo for an explanation of the strange sight, but his beautiful face was over-shadowed by a frown. Before her unspoken question he explained quietly, 'That church has been that way since 1944. After what happened there, it was decided never to rebuild. I'll take you there later. Then you will understand many things.'

Though the sun burned as brightly as ever, Antonia felt the shadow of distant tragedy pass over that beautiful day.

Chapter Six

Presently the car drew up before a massive wrought-iron gate between two ancient stone pillars, both adorned with stone carvings of the Quattromani crest. Lorenzo reached for a remote control inside the car, and the gates swung noiselessly open. A wide avenue took them through olive groves, and then through long rows of vines already groaning under the weight of their fruit.

'It will be a good vintage this year,' Lorenzo informed her proudly. 'Welcome to the home of the Gavedo grape.' The vines and the olive trees certainly looked prosperous enough, thought Antonia, but she had a growing sense of foreboding about this place, which had started with her glimpse of the abandoned church. Then, after a curve in the avenue, she caught sight of the castle of Gavedo, on an outcrop of rock looking down upon the vineyards. The castle only confirmed her feeling of desolation and sadness. She saw to her dismay that what had once been a building of some grandeur was now almost as decayed as the church she had just seen. In fact, it was sadder than many older ruins, because it bore signs of having been inhabited until relatively recently. It still had its roof, but it was broken in places, and beams poked through like the skeleton ribs of a rotting carcass.

'Oh, Lorenzo,' she sighed, 'what a terrible shame. Gianluca loved this place so much.'

Lorenzo chuckled softly. 'Yes, he would be ashamed of me, and quite rightly,' he admitted. 'I've managed to make the main walls of the building safe, but I've lacked the will to do anything else. If Giselle had wanted it for her cultural centre, then perhaps something could have been done with it, but no, nothing would do for her except Aunt's villa, and as you've seen, that's out of the question. Anyway, come and see. Who knows what ideas you might have.'

He drew up on a patch of level grass in front of the castle. Though there were signs that the building had been converted to gentler domestic use at a later date, there was no doubt that it had originally been intended to be a fortress. Even in its present forlorn condition, the castle presented a forbidding aspect to all comers. There was none of the refinement of the countess's villa, a monument to a later, more peaceful age. The castle rose strong and square, its thick outer walls having stood firm against the centuries. It was imposing, even in its derelict state.

'Come,' said Lorenzo and held out his hand. 'We'll look inside, but stay by me. Not all of the internal structure is sound.' He led her to a magnificent stone-carved doorway.

'This was cut into the medieval walls in the seventeenth century, when adjustments were made to turn this into a fine house. See, there's the Quattromani crest again above the lintel.' It was recognisable, but in a sorry state, chipped and with pieces flaking away. Lorenzo pushed the heavy studded door open, and its hinges creaked as if they felt pain. They walked across the threshold, and Antonia could not stifle a little cry of distress. All was abandonment and decay. Before them was the remains of what had been a grand marble staircase, but some of the marble slabs had been prised off and no doubt put to a more modest use, such as a farmhouse sink. Sconces for candles were still affixed to the walls of the staircase, but they were rusting away, streaking the plaster with orange. They looked as though they were bleeding to death. Antonia shivered. The beating of wings made her look up. High above, she could see where parts of the castle were open to the sky. Jagged, broken timbers creaked where the roof had fallen in, and birds flew in and out. There was rubble and fallen masonry everywhere.

'Let's go up,' Lorenzo said. 'But carefully.' He took her hand again, firmly, and led her slowly up the staircase. A doorway opened part of the way up, and they looked into a great hall. Some broken chairs still lay about either side of a huge fireplace Lorenzo could have stood up in. Some fuel still lay in the grate, but enterprising birds had taken it over as a rather grand nest. There were beautifully patterned tiles on the floor but it was as if they had given up trying to shine through the dust and decay. At the far end of the room another fine doorway opened into a further room.

'No,' murmured Lorenzo. 'I don't think we should go on. It probably isn't safe.'

Antonia nodded mutely, overcome by the melancholy air of the place. She felt relieved when they turned and descended the staircase again, Lorenzo holding her arm to steady her as they picked their way over fallen plaster and timbers. Once out of the castle, he did not let go of her, but slid his hand from her elbow to take her hand. This time he did not have the excuse of Antonia's safety for holding on to her, and she knew it. She hoped fervently that the warmth of her own hand within his firm grasp did not betray her nervousness.

'But where do you live then?' she asked.

'Oh, somewhere much less grand but a good deal more comfortable,' he reassured her. 'Let's walk there. We can come back for the car later.'

As they walked away from the sad ruin of one of Gianluca's favourite places, Lorenzo explained to her the seasons of the vine grower's year, the excitement of a great vintage and the way he had developed the international marketing of the Gavedo grape, using a worldwide network of wine merchants who had originally come from the area. He had truly turned a local industry into a thriving export business and was very proud that he made a significant contribution to local employment. As they walked they met a couple of estate workers, with whom he spent some minutes discussing some urgent business.

'I've a good team of people,' he explained. 'I know that they are able to handle most matters while I'm away.' A few minutes later he pointed out a sturdy stone farmhouse, shielded by vines, through which Antonia could just catch the blue glimmer of a swimming pool.

'There's my home,' he said. 'Hot and cold water inside, and cool outside.'

'Oh, I wish I'd brought a swimsuit!' she exclaimed.

'My fault, I should have said. What if I lend you some trunks and a tee-shirt? It wouldn't be very elegant but nobody would see you but me, and I can always promise not to look.'

An image flashed across her mind of a man standing below her window on a moonlit night, stripped the waist, looking up at her with a sad smile and a brief wave. He might promise not to look, but could she promise the same?

'Thank you, I'd like a swim. Won't you be having one too?' she asked, startled at her own unaccustomed forwardness, given what she was really thinking.

'Certainly, but I'll have one first, while you're getting ready,' he said.

He led her into the house. While the countess's villa was very grand but equally comfortable, this was comfortable in a simpler, more rustic way. The furniture was all of a sturdy country make, in keeping with style of the house, with its whitewashed walls and a few old Persian rugs spread out on the terracotta-tiled floors. A stone staircase in the corner led to the upper floor.

'Come up here,' said Lorenzo. 'I'll find you something.' Antonia followed him upstairs. Four doors led off one side of a corridor, as if the house were a small monastery. This impression was reinforced by the simplicity of the bedroom Lorenzo led her into. It was sparsely and simply furnished, and made Antonia think of a monastic cell, the room of a man who was used to living alone, of someone who preferred a solitary life. Lorenzo was rummaging in the drawers of an ancient, dark chest, finally pulling out a plain white tee-shirt and a pair of men's trunks.

'Try these,' he said, tossing them onto the bed. 'I'll see you downstairs. There's a little bathroom through there should you need one.' He indicated a door in the wall that Antonia had thought was a cupboard. Then he left her there.

Antonia stared down at the bed. So this was his room, the place where he slept when he was at home. A traditional white lace counterpane, the most ornate thing in the room, was thrown over the oak-framed bed. There were no pictures on the white walls, only a simple terracotta plaque of Mary and the baby Jesus. And yet he must sometimes bring Giselle to this austere room, she thought, and a sickening image flashed through her mind of his making love to her, heaving and panting, on that lovely counterpane. The purity of the room made the image more horrible and inappropriate.

Antonia tried to push these thoughts far from her mind. Giselle would only be away a month. *Enough! He has her, and I have my work. And besides, the countess counts on my loyalty.*

Yet Lorenzo had told her he did not love Giselle. Almost everything he said showed the widening gulf between them. Or was it all just a plot to gain her trust?

Antonia changed quickly, then went into the tiny bathroom to see what she looked like in the mirror. The trunks were baggy ones, like shorts, and Antonia decided that in spite of her shoulder-length hair she looked more like a dishevelled little boy than a twenty-five-year-old woman. A far cry from Giselle's tiny white bikini, she reminded herself bitterly.

The sound of a gentle splash came from the pool, so she hurried downstairs to join Lorenzo. She caught sight of him, lithe as an eel, gliding along under the surface of the water and she felt herself flame with longing for him.

He turned over again and swam with an easy stroke towards her, to stand in the water at the side of the pool. The water dripped from his raven-black hair and ran in rivulets down his chest.

'I thought you'd be ages yet – women so often are,' he said.

'Not this one,' she retorted, wishing he had not reminded her of his experience of other women, but she did not have it in her heart to be angry for long.

He climbed out of the water, smiling at her, and once more Antonia felt as overwhelmed by his beauty as she had been when they first met. Now she could observe him more closely than ever, the broadness of his muscular shoulders, the taut hardness of his stomach, the strong sinews of his muscled, hairy legs. His hard work under Alessio's guidance had honed his body until it was even more desirable than she had remembered it in the moonlight. Yet there was something naturally proportioned about his muscles – he looked that good because he worked hard, not because he worked out.

'Antonia!' he exclaimed, shattering her thoughts. 'You're looking at me as if you've never seen a man before!'

'Of course I have!' *Only, never one who looks like you.* 'But probably not as many as you've seen women.'

Lorenzo looked at her with a serious expression now. 'I like the way you look at me,' he said. To her surprise it was his turn to flush. Then he turned abruptly away from her and slid back into the water. 'Well, aren't you coming in then?' he asked, his head bobbing up again, sleek and gleaming as an otter's.

'Yes, of course!' She smiled at him, recovering her nerve, and jumped into the pool, where he started to splash her unmercifully. The water was delightfully cool on such a hot day, and Antonia relished the opportunity to stretch her whole body out, buoyed by the water. She started to swim lengths at a leisurely pace, enjoying an exercise she had not had in some time. She was hampered, however, by Lorenzo. His bronzed body bobbed in and out of the water like a porpoise, flashed under her like an eel, but tantalisingly he always just succeeded in not touching her.

'Lorenzo, you'd win prizes in a dolphinarium,' she exclaimed. He responded by hooting like a dolphin and flapping his hands together as if they were fins. Antonia had never seen him so relaxed, at home in his own world. Gradually she started to relax herself and to laugh and fool around in the water just as he was doing. Finally, they emerged and lay panting by the side of the pool. She closed her eyes and turned her face up to the sun.

'Oh Lorenzo, I don't think I've ever enjoyed myself so much,' she told him, and realised as she said it that it really was true. Her life had been such a lonely one. Lorenzo lay propped on one elbow, observing her through half-shut eyes. The coolness of the water had caused her nipples to harden and point and she knew he could not fail to notice how the tee-shirt and cotton trunks clung there and everywhere, revealing her body and yet not revealing it to him, in a way that was far more tantalising than the skimpiest bikini. He flopped over onto his stomach, but not before she had noticed the effect she was having on him.

'Hungry?' he asked.

'Oh yes,' she responded, her voice low and lazy in the heat. 'After that exercise, I could eat a horse!'

'Yes, well, I'm not partial to equine steak myself,' he said in a mock-serious tone, 'but there is a nice little trattoria in the village that has other things on the menu, and as for the wine they serve, let's just say it comes with a personal recommendation!'

'Sounds lovely.' She smiled.

'Go and rub yourself dry, then, before I come and do it for you,' he said, pretending to lunge at her. With a delighted squeak, Antonia jumped to her feet and ran into the house. It was only when she got into the little bathroom again and saw herself in the mirror that she realised what she looked like.

'Oh no,' she groaned. 'The classic wet tee-shirt routine. Imagine me falling for that.' However, she pulled the wet garment over her head and observed her naked breasts in the mirror, as her hair fell about her shoulders, already drying in the heat of the day. She cupped them for a moment in her palms, wondering in spite of herself what it would feel like to have Lorenzo's warm, strong, roughened hands there instead of her own. *I've never felt like this about anyone before, not even George. Especially not George.* She shuddered involuntarily at the thought of the fate she had so narrowly missed, wondering if the horror of those days would ever leave her. What was it about this country, this man who was so different from any other, that woke such strange, exhilarating feelings in her? Perhaps she would never be so happy again. Would it all end in tears?

'Antonia!' Lorenzo called up the stairs, breaking into her thoughts.

'Nearly ready,' she called back, though it was not strictly true. She hurried into her clothes, and within minutes they were setting off to where they had left the Mercedes by the deserted castle.

'Lorenzo,' she said impulsively as they approached the ruin, 'there are so many things you could do with this castle. Surely it's not too far gone. A study centre for wine, a Quattromani museum or just a place for holiday-makers, with grape picking thrown in, of course.'

'I knew you'd think of something,' he answered. 'All I've really lacked is the will and motivation to act. I'm sure you're right. It has withstood so many misfortunes without falling down completely that perhaps it can still be saved.'

They got back into the car, Antonia already wondering when, if ever, she would see the castle and Lorenzo's home again. They followed the road out of the estate and back to the straggling little village with the roofless church they had passed through earlier. Here Lorenzo led her to the charming little trattoria he had told her about. To allow diners to take advantage of the glorious weather, tables were laid out under a pergola grown over with vines. The proprietor clearly knew Lorenzo well and greeted him warmly, while he shook hands respectfully with Antonia.

'*Prego, accomodatevi,*' he said, indicating a table under the pergola. The people at the other tables appeared to be local, indeed many of them nodded to Lorenzo or greeted him by name. Although they tried to be discreet, Antonia could not miss the looks of curiosity they gave her.

'There are almost no tourists that come to this area,' Lorenzo said. 'I suppose it's a bit off the beaten track for them. I don't imagine there are many areas of Tuscany like it anymore. And no, I can tell from your face what you want to ask but never will. I don't bring Giselle here, not to this trattoria. It's far too simple for her tastes.'

Simple the food might have been, but it was delicious, a pasta course made with wild mushrooms, followed by a mixed grill of fish freshly caught in the Ligurian sea, and a light green salad. The wine, naturally, was Gavedo grape, a dry white that graced the simple trattoria just as easily as it did more illustrious tables in exclusive restaurants worldwide. Because he was driving, Lorenzo confined himself to one glass, following it with sparkling mineral water from the local spa high in the mountains.

Antonia stared out in a sweet haze of contentment at the beauty of the lush green valley, the majesty of the mountains rising above them, and almost without thinking she said dreamily, 'I don't think I have ever had such a perfect day.'

'Nor have I,' came his answer, slow and serious. She turned and looked at him and could see from his face that he meant it.

'Come,' he said gravely. 'There is something else I must show you. Then we should go back and see how Aunt is getting on.'

It seemed natural now to put her hand into his

outstretched one, and they walked out together into the dappling sunshine. A stab of irrational jealousy shot through her. This place might not be fancy enough for Giselle, but who knew how many other women he had brought to this spot before her? Had he been equally gallant with them?

He was leading her away from the cluster of houses and up towards the little abandoned church just outside the village. Then he said, 'I've never brought anyone here. It's a tragic and shameful spot, but not everyone can appreciate that.'

They passed among the graves, all beautifully tended, all bearing little oval photographs of their owners, in keeping with the Mediterranean tradition. At first Antonia had the impression that most of the villagers had died young, until she realised that most of them had chosen youthful photographs so that they would be commemorated at their best. Then she saw what Lorenzo had brought her here for. On the side wall of the abandoned shell of the church he silently pointed out three more such photographs, mounted with the names of their owners on a little marble plaque. All three were young men, all three had died on the same day in 1944. Suddenly Antonia realised why the otherwise smooth stone of the church wall was pitted here and there with deep holes. Years of weathering could not disguise the fact that the three young partisans had been buried, and were now commemorated, on the spot where they had been shot. Her eyes brimmed with tears.

'Come,' he murmured, placing his hand gently on her waist as he led her gently to where the main door of the church had been. They walked through the arch in the wall together. The bare walls of the interior of the building were scorched and blackened.

'After they'd been shot, their killers torched everything. It was the right thing not to rebuild. This is their memorial,' Lorenzo continued in a voice grim with pain. 'Some of the perpetrators stood trial and were imprisoned, and when they got out of gaol they never came back here. But the people here know who was behind the ambush – they know it was my father's work. He pretended to be a partisan only long enough to betray his trusting comrades to the fascists. This is my inheritance, Antonia.'

She wept for the three lives tragically cut short, wept for the countess for the pain she still suffered, and wept for herself and the futile love she now knew, beyond a doubt, that she had for this man. Then she felt his arms about her – her cheek lay against his shirt, his heart beating fast under the cool fabric.

'*Antonia mia, tesoro, non piangere.* Don't cry, my treasure,' he murmured against her hair. She did not have to understand all of his words to know that they were words of comfort.

As they started their journey back across the mountains, the shimmering heat of the day became heavy and oppressive. Dark and threatening clouds wreathed the mountain peaks and spread across the sky. Something in nature had to give, and finally it came, an earth-shattering bolt of lightning in the now purple sky, followed in an instant by an angry roll and clap of thunder. Then the rain came, rod-straight upon the curving road, in warm, heavy drops which steamed on the tarmac.

'The gods are angry,' Lorenzo joked.

'What have we done to make them angry?' she countered.

'Oh, I don't know,' he shrugged. 'Perhaps we forgot to make them a sacrifice. Feel like volunteering?' he added wickedly.

Antonia laughed, and saw an answering laugh in his slate-grey eyes. In that split second of distraction the accident happened. The Mercedes was poised to take a tight, upward bend in the road when towards them slewed a huge articulated lorry. It had lost its grip in the wet and was coming as though in slow motion to their side of the road. She saw the terrified face of the driver, his mouth open, but the screaming she heard was her own. The impact when it came jolted her in every bone. By then she had already shut her eyes and started to pray. Then an unearthly quiet descended, broken only by the sound of the relentless driving rain. Antonia's face was streaming with tears, her body wracked with great, soundless sobs. Then she felt herself encircled by Lorenzo's protecting arms.

'Oh my darling, it's all right, *va tutto bene*. Don't cry, *mia cara*, don't cry.' Then she felt his mouth brush her forehead, her eyelids, her cheeks, gentle moth-touches to soothe away the tears. His hands trembled at her neck and shoulders. The gods might have been angry, but this time they had shown mercy.

Apart from the shock, they were unscathed. The bonnet of the big car was crushed and wedged in behind the front and middle wheels of the lorry. Its driver, too, had been lucky, high up in his cab. Antonia watched him slowly open his door and pause there, as if he were afraid of the short distance he had to step down. Gingerly, as if he did not quite believe he was in one piece and might fall to bits if he moved too quickly, the man stepped down onto the road. It was there that the shock hit him. He crouched down on the tarmac, wrapped his arms around himself and started to moan like a wounded animal.

From somewhere inside the wrecked Mercedes Lorenzo retrieved his mobile. Antonia was aware that as he dialled the emergency services his hands were still shaking, but otherwise he appeared to be completely in control. Before long an ambulance and the carabinieri had arrived and the still terrified driver was wrapped in a blanket and helped off the road. Antonia's side of the Mercedes was relatively undamaged, and she was dimly aware of the door opening and hands reaching for her. All her instincts were to stay in the protecting circle of Lorenzo's arms until she heard his voice gently urging her to go.

'Go with them. It'll be all right. I'll be with you soon.'

As she allowed herself to be helped out of the wreckage, she realised from their familiar, reassuring smiles that this was the same crew who had come to take the countess to hospital the day of her fall.

'The countess!' she gasped, realising that she had completely forgotten their promised visit, and that if they saw the old lady today it would be under entirely different circumstances. She caught sight of Lorenzo through the relentless rain, his clothes clinging to him and his hair as slickly wet as when he had emerged from the swimming pool. He was in earnest conversation with the carabinieri and she understood from his gestures that he was explaining how the accident had happened. Minutes later he joined her in the waiting ambulance, putting his arms around her where she sat huddled in a blanket.

'My darling girl,' he murmured softly, 'I'm so sorry.'

'Don't say that,' she exclaimed. 'There was nothing you could have done. We should just be thankful we've all had such a lucky escape. If you hadn't turned the wheel away just as you did, we wouldn't have been this lucky. And Lorenzo,' she added, looking up at him with shining eyes, 'I shall always remember this as the most extraordinary day of my entire life.'

'So will I,' he answered her slowly, 'and not because of this accident.'

'How different from our normal visit,' remarked Lorenzo

gently, as the ambulance swung through the gates of the little hospital in the early evening light. After they had been thoroughly checked over by emergency room staff, Antonia and Lorenzo were free to go.

'Let me call the villa just to let Luigi know what's happening, and then we'll go and see Aunt,' he said. Antonia nodded mutely. Lorenzo spoke quietly for a few minutes on his mobile. 'Luigi will come to fetch us in an hour. I've no car for the time being, after all. We'll be marooned at the villa for a while.'

'You make it sound just like one of Gianluca's adventures,' said Antonia with a sad smile.

'Come on, it's time we told my aunt about what we've been up to – though I might leave out some of the details,' he said with a wink.

Laura Quattromani was already back in bed for the night when they walked into her ward, but she lay with her face turned towards the wall. Gradually she turned to look at them, and it wrenched Antonia's heart to see the signs of recent tears. Clearly the news had already reached her.

'Come here, my dear,' she whispered, and stretched out her old arms to embrace her. 'Thank heavens you're all right, my poor child.' The countess held her tight for some moments before she said in a stronger voice. 'You love him.'

Antonia stiffened with surprise in the old lady's embrace. 'I guessed this was coming from your face that morning you came to breakfast, the day we went to Dante's tower. You love him,' she repeated, 'body and soul. It shines out of your eyes. You,' she said, over Antonia's shoulder, 'you'd better show you're worthy of her!'

The old arms gradually loosened their grip. Antonia lifted her head to face the countess, her face burning. She neither confirmed nor denied the old lady's words. There was no need to. Lorenzo stood just behind them. He had not spoken since they entered the ward, but now he broke his silence.

'I love her, Aunt. I will prove myself worthy of her.' And with that, he left the ward.

Suddenly Antonia was overcome. He had said they should tell the whole truth, but this she had not expected. It was all too much for her, the extremes of emotion she had experienced that day, the breathtaking majesty of the landscape, the melancholy crumbling grandeur of Gavedo castle, the beauty of Lorenzo's near-naked body glimpsed through the sparkling water, the joy of being in his company unlike any joy she had ever known, the horror of the burned-out church, their own escape from death, and finally, this unexpected declaration. All her pent-up emotion spilled out of her in a flood of tears as she leaned her head against the countess's shoulder. But there was relief in her tears too, relief that Laura Quattromani knew her secret. The old lady stroked her hair softly, and her touch gave Antonia inexpressible comfort. She cried on and on, until her body felt as though it had been wrung out of tears and she shook with exhaustion.

'Go to him, my child. And stop crying – though shock has something to do with it. You should be happy. I pray with all my heart that he means what he says, for all our sakes. Now go, go,' the countess urged her.

'Until tomorrow?' asked Antonia falteringly, fearful of refusal.

'I should think so,' answered the countess, a hint of her old liveliness coming back. 'Poor Gianluca has been abandoned today. Be sure that you've something to report tomorrow.'

Antonia smiled through her tears, squeezed the old lady's hands and walked out of the ward to where Lorenzo was waiting for her.

'Let me take you home,' he murmured, and led her, without speaking, through the hospital to the entrance where Luigi was patiently waiting for them in his battered old Cinquecento. Antonia was touched by the concern on Luigi's face.

'Elena and I were so worried,' he said. 'It's such a relief to see you well. She has some homemade soup for you both if you could manage some.'

'I'd love that,' Antonia said warmly.

'So would I,' added Lorenzo, as they got into the little car.

After their simple supper he left Antonia at the foot of the stairs.

'I love you, Antonia. I knew it from the moment I saw

the vision of your face framed in your window. Only in that moment did I realise what love really is. All my life I'd thought love was a commodity, to be bought and sold. I confused love with the search for temporary pleasure. I'd never really known love, only the love my nanny showed me when I was a little boy.'

In the gathering dusk she looked down at his upturned face from where she stood two steps up and seemed to see in the face of the man the shadowy face of the lonely child.

He went on, 'I was only waiting to love you for my life to slot into place. Thirty-two years I've lived without knowing it, but now I have a goal in life, a reason for everything I do. Whatever happens, my love for you will always be there. It's here, in the bricks and mortar of this house, it's in every drop of my own wine, it's in these mountains that surround us. Can you imagine how I felt when suddenly I saw you in the moonlight, knew you were my destiny, and that I might have already lost you? All I had done up to then was to make fun of you, to insult you. You must have despised me, and you had every right to.'

Antonia was about to speak when he came up a step, until their faces were level, and laid a finger gently against her lips.

'Say nothing now, my darling,' he urged her softly. 'Let me prove myself to you.' With these final words his lips brushed hers, and then he melted away into the shadows.

Antonia turned and mounted the stairs slowly, her mind

in turmoil. Everything was happening so fast. When finally she slipped into her bed, her last conscious thought before sleep overtook her was that she was a different person from the one who had woken that morning.

Chapter Seven

Over the next few days, their lives outwardly followed the same routine as before, but everything else had changed. When they met at breakfast, Lorenzo would rise to greet her, meet her lips with his for a moment in a tantalisingly brief embrace, and then lead her to her chair. His was an old-fashioned, discreet courtship. After breakfast he would then head off to work with Alessio and the other estate employees. Antonia worked steadily at her cataloguing – she could see the end in sight. Soon her work would be ready to share with the state archive in Florence. After lunch she often took a nap on her private terrace, or a gentle walk along the paths of the estates. Sometimes Lorenzo would accompany her, holding her hand or gently encircling her waist. Antonia had never known such exquisite happiness, but she knew she was holding her breath emotionally. How long could such happiness last? And why was he holding back? *I daren't run at him. I'm afraid of spoiling everything.* Sometimes she thought it must be too good to be true, as if the villa must be enchanted and she too was under its spell.

In the evenings Luigi lent them his rattling little Cinquecento to go to the hospital, since the Mercedes was still being repaired.

'I think I enjoy driving this old banger more than all those high-end motors I've always had, even if finding space for my knees is a bit a problem,' Lorenzo told her, raising his voice because the windows were open.

'I can see that,' she said. 'You look younger.'

'That's not just the car, Antonia!'

The countess always received their news with eagerness, but Antonia could see that the old lady was not merely listening to the words they spoke to her but also reading all the language of their looks and gestures. Antonia could see the countess was cautious, though. She wasn't quite ready to give them her blessing.

'Give her time,' Lorenzo urged her. 'She's so fond of you, of course she's not sure yet. I haven't exactly been a model of good behaviour when it comes to women, after all.'

Antonia could not keep the hurt from her face.

'Oh my darling, I'm sorry! That's all in the past now,' he soothed her, tracing a fingertip over her trembling lip. 'I mean to convince you of that, and Aunt too.'

A few days after the accident, Lorenzo again took Antonia for a day out, a shorter trip this time. Because they were again relying on Luigi's old car, it was a characterful rather than a comfortable ride. On this occasion they went to visit a hilltop church perched above a neighbouring town.

The place was deserted except for the scurrying of ever-present lizards, and they sat down in the warm, dry grass of the hillside amongst the gently nodding poppies to admire the view. The distant murmur of the little town rose up to where they sat – muffled bells, the hum of the occasional car or roar of a motor-scooter. It was a hot, still day, and Antonia felt relaxed and drowsy. She lay back in the grass, feeling it crinkling against her spine, and with her eyes shut she turned her face up at the sun and stretched as languidly as a cat.

'Ah, you shouldn't do that!' Lorenzo warned her, and she opened her eyes to see his dark face silhouetted against the light.

'You are quite irresistible,' he continued. 'I can't be held responsible for my actions.'

'Hey. Anyone and everyone is responsible for his actions.'

'Sorry. I'm learning, honestly.'

Yet he seemed to her to have gone to the opposite extreme, as if she was a piece of Meissen china that might break if not handled correctly. His restraint, since telling her how he felt, puzzled and tantalised her. What had happened to the Lorenzo who had held her close and comforted her in the burned-out church? Where, even, was the uncompromising Lorenzo who had been so determined that first afternoon in the chapel? It was almost as though he was holding back, trying to prove he could be different. Yet all the emerging woman in her now wanted was to see his face closer and closer to her own until he blotted out the sun, to feel the weight of his tensed body on her own, the urgency of his desire.

She lay now in the grass with her hands placed one above the other, resting on her waist. Then, barely conscious of what she was doing, she opened her arms and stretched them out in the grass on either side of her head.

This time Lorenzo let go of his self-control. With a low cry of passion his head dipped to hers, his body curved above hers, and with his hands he pinned hers to the ground, though she offered him no resistance.

Half in a swoon she felt his mouth on hers and parted her lips gently at the urging of his insistent tongue. Experienced lover that he was, he knew how to tease her further to heighten her longing. His tongue flickered in her mouth for an instant, and then she felt his teeth gently nibble at the corner of her mouth before they moved softly to her ear, then down to her throat. Antonia heard herself moan in spite of herself, overcome with desire, and as if he had been waiting for that signal, his body covered hers. Her knees gave way beneath his urgent pressure and gently parted, and the thin cotton of her dress did nothing to conceal from her the heat and hardness of his want.

At last his mouth again fell greedily on hers, his darting tongue touched hers, and that instinct that until so recently she had not known she possessed made her free her hands from his grasp and cup his tense, muscular buttocks, urging his body against hers in its irresistible, rhythmic movement. Lorenzo moved a now-free hand to her breast, alternatively kneading it and flicking gently at the nipple, which pushed hard through her light bra and the summer cotton of her dress. After what seemed a delicious eternity, he raised a face suffused with passion to hers and looked down at her where she lay flushed and panting.

'I love you, Antonia,' he murmured.

'And I love you, Lorenzo, and I want you.' The words came out before she knew it, responding to the cry of her body.

He said nothing more, but without ever moving his eyes from her face, he started to unbutton her dress with a sure and practised hand. Presently he pushed the fabric back from her shoulders and slid his hands under her as she arched her back for him, unhooking her bra. Then, pulling away the loosened clothes from her upper body, he at last looked down at her naked breasts and let out a groan of admiration.

'I imagined you so many times, but never so beautiful as this,' he said in a voice husky and ragged with emotion. 'And I love you to look at me,' she answered, with tears caught in her throat.

He took a nipple between finger and thumb and started to caress it gently, teasingly. His touch seemed to reach the core of her being, and just when she thought the pleasure was almost too much for her to bear, his mouth covered her taut nipple and he started to suck, gently moving his tongue over its surface while his hand teased gently at her other breast. All her habitual restraint gave way as Antonia pushed her hips hard against him, letting out a low cry almost of pain. She cast all caution away. She wanted him, he wanted her, and neither could think of anything else. 'I want you!' she repeated.

Suddenly all the bells in the little town down below in the valley broke into a cacophonous peal, running up and down the scales more in haste than in time. Every car horn in the place started to sound at once, the noise echoing back and forth amongst the surrounding hills.

Lorenzo raised his head and gave a low laugh of joy. 'There's a good omen,' he said.

'What do you mean?' stammered Antonia, half in this world, half still in the private world of their passion. He propped himself on one elbow and smiled down at her.

'It's a wedding,' he explained. 'We always make that din, so you'll need to get used to the idea. We will of course need to discuss what else we want to happen,' and he laid a hand proprietorially on her naked breast. Antonia's flesh tingled again at his touch.

'I don't understand,' she whispered, half-afraid of what he might say next.

'Antonia,' he said, serious now, 'I meant what I said about wanting to be worthy of you. You know that I want to be inside you, to possess you completely.' He paused for a moment, and she shivered – at his words, at the thought of a pleasure that frightened her by its promised intensity. Then he went on, and she sensed him searching her face for the effect of his words.

'But I don't just mean now, here, on this hillside. I mean in my bed at Gavedo, under my aunt's roof, in my castle when we've rebuilt it, everywhere, in fact, that we may find ourselves in this life. I want every morning to see your face on my pillow, your hair tumbled about, be it this lovely rich colour,' and he wound some of it around his hand, 'or one day streaked with grey. I want you forever. I want to marry you, Antonia. Nothing else will do.'

Antonia gazed at him, wondering, as gradually the force of his words brought her back to her senses. Marry him! The thought terrified her, not because she did not want him, but because she was afraid again that this was all too unreal. She remembered as if it were yesterday returning all those wedding presents that had been given to her and George, putting a 'wedding dress, never worn,' on eBay, then as quickly withdrawing it from sale and posting it without a return address to the nearest Oxfam bridal shop, far enough away for her not to see the dress on display, or worse, coming out of a church door to a shower of confetti. She remembered the sidelong glances, the gossip, then the reporters camped on the doorstep, the river of hate that surged onto her social media, from people she had never met, saying, 'You must have known.' She'd taken down her profiles before she'd drowned in that sewage. George had seemed so sure, so dependable, everything in fact that Lorenzo had appeared not to be at first, and look what had happened. And here she was after a few days, listening to this man telling her he wanted to marry her.

Antonia sat up suddenly and then realised that she was still half-naked under his burning gaze. In confusion she tried to cover herself up.

'Don't, Antonia. Leave those buttons. You're too lovely to be covered up.' He grasped both her hands and covered her palms with kisses. Then holding both her wrists with one strong hand he unbuttoned his own shirt.

'Touch me, Antonia – please,' he said, releasing her.

She stroked her palms against the drift of silky hair on his breastbone. How alive he was.

'Feel my heart beating.'

She could not ignore it, feeling it thudding against her hand. Her own was beating so loudly she felt sure that he too must be able to hear it.

'I love you, Lorenzo. I've never felt like this before. You'd better not be teasing me,' she cried, tears starting to come despite her efforts at self-control. In an instant his arms were around her, her breasts crushed against his chest in the force of his embrace.

'Tease you? My darling, no. You give me a happiness I've never known. How could I ever want to hurt you?' He kissed her forehead, soothed her shuddering sobs. 'I'm sorry,' he murmured, 'I've been too fast for you, I've frightened you.'

'No, Lorenzo, don't say that. I wanted you to touch me the way you did this afternoon. I still do, you must know that. I'm just so afraid of this bubble bursting, this exquisite happiness coming to an end, and now you talk of marriage.'

'This is no bubble waiting to burst. That's precisely why I'm asking you to marry me. I don't want you to get away. I want the happiness to last forever. So don't be frightened.' He put a finger under her chin and tilted her tear-stained face up to his.

'Is it Giselle you're worried about?' he asked her softly. She shook her head mutely, then nodded it, then shook it again in confusion. She had been thinking of Giselle, and other things.

'Well, don't worry,' he reassured her. 'I'm going to call her and tell her it's all over between us. It's been over actually for a long time, that is if we ever really got started. She never really cared for me. I think I just suited her, and I know I've never been in love until now. I'm thirty-two years old, Antonia. I'm very rich, extremely privileged. I've had plenty of opportunities, and have taken them, although I've always been safe, responsible. Some of the opportunities, I have to confess, were not strictly mine to take, other men's bored wives, that sort of thing. I always thought that if I was discreet, took precautions and so on, that I could go on forever like that. I know it pains you to hear me say that, but I want to be absolutely honest with you. I want you to have no illusions. That used to be me.' He smiled for a moment before he went on. 'Then you came along and changed all of that. I don't want to behave like that now. It simply doesn't interest me anymore. From the start you were different from all those others. What a dent to my silly pride it was that day when you pushed me away. You brought me to my senses.'

Antonia started to smile through her tears, her sobs subsiding.

'I've rushed you,' he went on. 'But we don't have to marry in a hurry if you don't want to. I know you want to convince my aunt that I mean what I say about wanting to be worthy of you. I want you to be my wife. Ask anything of me, ask me anything about my life up to now. There's plenty I'm not proud of, but you have the right to know all of it if you want. Is there anything you want to tell me?' he added, his eyes searching her face. She looked away from his gaze and was silent.

'So there is something, even in your life,' he murmured. 'But nothing matters now except that we are together. We're adults. I've lived my life, you've lived yours. And I love you for the person you are now.'

Antonia looked up at him, and when she spoke it was in a firm, steady voice.

'I was engaged to be married once, but it ended badly. I thought I loved him, though now I know differently. I was affectionate and loyal towards him, probably too loyal.'

'He let you down?' asked Lorenzo.

'Yes and no. He turned out not to be the person I thought he was. You're going to think this is really weird. He and I were never lovers. I thought we would be once we got engaged. You see, I didn't really have what most people my age think of as a normal adolescence. I don't mean I was a complete innocent – I wasn't. In fact after a bit I thought perhaps *he* thought I was, but the longer that went on the more difficult it was to tell him I wasn't. Am I making sense?'

'You are. But the man was a fool.'

'It would have been all right if that's all he was, Lorenzo. I think I'd probably have broken it off even if matters hadn't, as you might say, intervened – I mean, if George hadn't been arrested.'

'Arrested?'

'I'll come to that. My problem was that I didn't have anyone to guide me. Mum fell ill in my fourth year of high school, and she was dead before I met George. I was a bit trapped. I mean, living in a small town where everyone knew whenever I sneezed. But I loved my job. In some ways I was very mature – or perhaps just too serious for my own good. I thought I had to be sensible. Being with George, on the face of it, looked sensible. Only then I found out what he really was.'

'Do you want to talk about it?' he asked quietly.

'Oh yes, yes I do. I never really have, you see. I've just bottled it up. It was a terrible time,' she murmured. Suddenly she remembered her naked breasts and said, 'How strange this is – because it isn't strange …'

'Whatever do you mean?'

'I mean lying here like this, half-undressed, and talking to you like this. It feels natural, somehow.'

'Because it is. I wonder how many people born in these valleys were conceived just like this, lying in the grass of a sunny afternoon. But I want to be tantalised for just a little bit longer. I want to make love to you and fall asleep in your arms, and wake up beside you, with no pressure to be anywhere else. I want you in my bed. But first I want you to face whatever is hiding in the shadows, and let us chase it out together.'

Antonia took a deep breath. 'Everyone said George was a catch, very dependable, very considerate. But something troubled me. I found out that his own mother, unfriendly though she was to me, to everybody, was afraid of him, though I couldn't see why. She was a battle-axe, and no mistake. I'd emailed a friend in London, telling her I was engaged and though we hadn't set the date, asking her on the quiet if she'd be my bridesmaid, or rather, matron of honour, as she's already married with a little girl. Jane's husband is in the police, a detective in fact, and it can only be divine providence that he had just recently been assigned to the Vice Squad, though at the time it was all such a terrible shock.' Antonia felt the blood drain beneath her tan and her hand, enclosed in Lorenzo's stronger one, trembled.

He squeezed it gently, and reassured, she went on.

'The squad had recently raided a particularly notorious club in Soho. The poor girls who worked there were exploited terribly. Some were trafficked immigrants who had no choice, they were slaves, really, while others were teenage runaways. Many of them had been in care, very vulnerable and prepared to accept anything in order to get a roof over their heads. Once into that life, it was virtually impossible to get out. Jane's husband, Simon, wouldn't talk about all the details, but he did say that the girls' bruises were regularly covered up with theatrical makeup. Not that they often tried to argue with the gang who ran the club – it just wasn't worth it. I lived in London myself while I was studying, but you can live in a place and never know what it's really like just below the surface. Jane's husband infiltrated the club by posing as a customer, going to the shows there, getting to know the regulars …'

'And one of them turned out to be your fiancé,' muttered Lorenzo, his face dark with anger.

'Not quite. Worse than that. He was one of the partners – associates, as the police put it. He was profiting from that misery. Had been for five years or so. I don't know how he got into it. It wasn't as if I went up to the Old Bailey – the court – to follow the trial, though I think it might have been through a contact he had had at law school who made what you might call a "business proposition." But you know, I'm just so thankful that even London can be a small world sometimes. Simon, Jane's husband, managed to uncover evidence that drugs were being sold through the club and pushed onto those poor girls, as if they weren't slaves enough already. He had clear evidence already that the club owners were living off immoral earnings, because he had got into the confidence of one of the youngest girls there. She grew to trust him because he never tried to touch her but would just buy time to talk to her. She was a very courageous young woman, in spite of her situation. Her testimony in court was crucial in getting those men convicted. Well, the investigation took some months, but finally the place was raided in a joint operation between the Vice and the Drug squads, and all the ringleaders were arrested. George got eight years. They also tracked what he was doing online – through the dark web, I mean. That would have been enough to put him away on its own. He even wrote to me saying he was sorry and wanted to explain everything, trying to claim he had some kind of illness, like an addiction, and could I go and visit him in Brixton.'

'*Dio mio*. What happened to the girl who gave evidence?' asked Lorenzo.

'When it was all over she went back to her home town, in the north-west of England. She received a lot of counselling – she needed it – and now she's back at college and plans to become a nurse. She told Simon that she wanted to care for people because so few people had ever cared for her and she wanted to make up for that.'

'What goodness to come out of all that squalor,' he murmured.

'It's often that way. People can be so quick to judge girls like her, when the truth is they're often the powerless tools of ruthless men. Other girls took courage from the example set by that one girl, and they too testified in the end. Those girls who had charges against them had them dropped because of their cooperation. The judge agreed that they had already suffered enough.'

'You never went to Brixton to see him, I trust?'

'Never. I never responded to him at all. But more men should have been punished. All the customers in the club were stopped and questioned. You'd be really surprised at who some of them were. Fine upstanding members of the community. Hypocrites, more like. But they never faced charges. Simon gave evidence against George in court. He said that when he was working undercover George had boasted to him about his Jekyll and Hyde existence. He'd bragged about what a successful person he was, a big fish in a small pond, sneering about all those people who thought highly of him in our small town. H-he even talked about me ...' Her voice dropped to a whisper. 'He thought he was showing off to a man as depraved as himself that he was going to marry an innocent little librarian and teach her all he knew.'

'Oh, my poor Antonia,' Lorenzo said, in a voice which trembled with compassion and anger at the same time. He leaned over and sheltered her in his arms.

'Do you see how lucky I was? Simon got my details when he impounded George's computer and phone. You can imagine his shock when he realised that George's librarian was me. He drove down from London to speak to me face to face rather than leave the follow-up to the local force. I thought the bottom had dropped out of my world. I mean, really, it felt like the ground was moving under my feet.' Her voice faded for a moment and when she spoke again it was with deadly calm. 'Once it had sunk in, all sorts of things fell into place. It wasn't just that odd feeling about him I had had sometimes. There were those weekends away that he told me were business trips, though he was very close about what he did on them. And what business would a solicitor in a market town in the West Country have to do in London so often?' Antonia's voice trailed away. She felt suddenly that she was light-years away from this beautiful landscape. Only the pressure of Lorenzo's comforting arms brought her back to the present.

'Did you have to testify?' he asked.

'No. The police already had overwhelming evidence. I was mentioned in court, apparently, though not by name I think, just to show how duplicitous he was. Men like George will always exist, and there will always be people for them to exploit. But though I'd done nothing wrong and there was lots of sympathy for me, especially from his mother, I felt so humiliated that I didn't want to stay in that town. I really couldn't stand that everyone knew I'd been taken in, though in a way he'd taken in everyone, not just me. And of course I couldn't get to work for about a fortnight. There were reporters there every time I opened the front door and every time I opened my laptop.'

'Vultures.'

'The police were very good – they kept moving them on, but the journos kept slithering back. They lost interest only when some cabinet minister was stupid enough to send intimate pictures of himself to an intern. Off they went to make the minister's wife have an even worse time than she was having already. Then I saw your aunt's advertisement and took the opportunity to escape.'

'Oh my poor Antonia, I've been so thoughtless,' Lorenzo said sadly. 'The day you met me you must have thought – what is it you say? – that you had got out of the frying pan and into the fire.'

'I'd love it, though, if you were one day to meet my dear old boss, Arthur. He was like a father to me. Much more of a father than the one I should have had, in fact,' she sighed.

'Yes, I'd like to meet him, this Arthur. You've seen me in my natural habitat, but I know so little of yours,' he said.

'You would?' She smiled up at him.

'Why not?'

She got up, brushing down her clothes. 'Come on, we'd better go. We're due at the hospital. Oh, I keep forgetting. I'm all undone.'

'Let me deal with that,' said Lorenzo, reaching round her to hook up her bra. 'I want the practice – I mean, to get better at wrapping and unwrapping this particular little parcel.'

A gentle breeze wafted her hair across her face, so she knew he couldn't see her expression as he reminded her gently, 'I don't have an answer yet.'

She brushed her hair out of her eyes, smiling.

'An answer? Yes. Of course it's yes. But I think I must be dreaming. If I am, don't wake me up.'

'Even with a kiss?'

Two days later the countess came home, a bit stiff and sore still, but definitely on the road to recovery. Her return coincided with the return of the Mercedes from the body shop, looking as if it had never suffered so much as a scratch in its entire life.

'Well, we've both of us had spare parts fitted, so we're both as good as new,' joked the countess to Antonia. 'I'm glad the Mercedes is back, because if I've to see the physiotherapist every other day it's going to be a much more comfortable ride than in the Cinquecento.'

'I'll come with you,' said Antonia.

'No you won't. I'd be happier knowing you were working on the archive instead. Gianluca must be angry enough at me already for being clumsy enough to fall down those steps,' she insisted. 'So let's not waste any more of his time. My nephew will take me. It'll give me an opportunity to grill him on whatever he intends to do with his life. And that, my dear, is probably better done when you are not present, don't you think? No need for that blushing, Antonia …'

Lorenzo carefully tucked his aunt into the small car, then slid into the driver's seat for the first of her trips to the physiotherapist.

'Well,' exclaimed Laura Quattromani, 'I may not be completely sound in wind and limb, but there's nothing wrong with my brain. And certainly not with my powers of observation,' she added as she tapped her nephew's knee. 'That girl is in love with you, Lorenzo. Now, what are you going to do about it?'

'What do you think, Aunt?' he cried in exasperation. 'I want to marry her.'

'Oh you do, do you?' Her eyes went round with mock surprise. 'And what, pray, is Antonia's response to that?'

'She'll have me. I hope you're pleased, Aunt.'

'I think you're luckier than you deserve. Just make sure you don't take her for granted. You'll have me to answer to if you do.'

'I'll never do that.'

'I think I've misjudged you, Lorenzo,' said Laura in a gentler tone. 'There's someone in you I didn't think existed.'

Lorenzo glanced at her quickly, then back at the road.

'If that's true,' he said, 'the credit is Antonia's.'

'No doubt you're right, in part at least. But no woman

alive can reform a man who doesn't want to be reformed,' she answered shrewdly.

They were approaching the gates of the hospital when the old lady spoke the words which Lorenzo knew would calm Antonia's fears and his own. 'You'll have to give me time, Lorenzo, to get used to this. I feel very protective towards Antonia. She's alone in the world, and I was responsible for bringing her out to Italy, and in a sense, for throwing her in your path.'

Lorenzo thought of the path he had taken to the little chapel that first day, and his hands tightened imperceptibly on the wheel.

'But I am sure,' continued his aunt, 'that in due course you will have my blessing. Just treat her properly, and for goodness sake, make your peace with that Landsdorf woman before she causes any more trouble.'

'Oh, don't worry. I've already written to her explaining everything. I was going to call her, but I'll confess I lost my nerve. In a way, I'm sorry to have taken an easy way out. Ideally I would rather have seen her face to face. But I'm sure she never really loved me anyway. It'll give her the chance to find someone in New York if she wants, with an easy conscience. She probably won't even get in touch. Nothing will get in the way of Antonia and me now. Nothing.'

The countess looked at him sharply. 'I wouldn't be so sure,' was all she said.

Chapter Eight

The atmosphere in the villa at mealtimes was now relaxed and friendly. Antonia admired the countess' evident determination that no matter if she was slow in getting about, her mood and quick wit were going to make up for it. Antonia was grateful that the countess was a good employer, refusing to take advantage of Antonia's willingness to spend long hours at work. She also seemed to want to make up for any earlier reluctance to accept the undeniable love of Lorenzo for Antonia.

'There's more to life than Quattromani archives,' she announced. 'Spend time with a living Quattromani instead. Gianluca would hardly mind. My nephew needs the stimulus of intelligent female company. He has to make up for a lot of lost time,' she added darkly.

One particularly happy evening, about a week after she came home from hospital, the old lady got up from the dinner table and said, 'I'm going to bed early.'

Antonia was startled. 'Are you all right?'

'Never felt better ... well, not quite that, perhaps, but

you know what I mean.'

'Do you need any help?' Antonia spoke to Laura's retreating back.

'None whatsoever! I've a book to read.' She stomped off, leaving Lorenzo and Antonia looking at each other. There was no mistaking Lorenzo's smile.

'We've passed the test, Antonia,' he said. 'Let's go for a walk, and then ...'

They strolled hand in hand around the ornamental garden of the villa. The twilight was alive with the chirping of crickets, but the only other sounds were the whinnying of a restless thoroughbred in his stall, the scuttling of tiny animals in the gathering gloom, the gentle splash of the fountain with its merry figure of Cupid. These days the little bronze figure seemed to Antonia to smile more than ever.

'The god of love,' said Lorenzo. 'Useless to try to resist his arrows.' He pulled her close and kissed her. When at last they drew back and looked into each other's eyes, the light was fading into a glorious gold-red sunset. Tomorrow would be another fine day, another day in their lives together.

'This is paradise,' she insisted to him.

'Anywhere would be paradise, like this,' he murmured, and pulling her to him he gently grazed on her mouth again. She tightened her arms about his neck, feeling the warmth of his hard chest and the urgent beating of his heart against her breasts. One of his hands stole up to caress their firm outline, so gently that she thought she would faint from desire. Then slowly he unbuttoned the top few buttons of her dress and traced with his finger a line from her throat down to her cleft. Antonia's breath caught in her throat as he eased her dress back over her shoulders and gently lifted each breast from the confines of her bra. His mouth brushed her lips again rapidly, then moved to her ears, her neck, and downwards until he found his mark at each hardening nipple. Antonia felt as though the blood was leaving her brain, leaving her faint as it flowed instead to where his tongue insistently worked, making her nipples so sensitive they were almost painful. She knew instinctively that for both of them there was only one way to assuage that sweet pain. Her flesh tingled at the soft touch of his hair. A low moan tore from her. 'Lorenzo, Lorenzo,' she whispered.

He raised his head, laughing softly, and momentarily caught her open mouth with his before again travelling slowly downwards. But after some moments of delicious, gentle teasing, he lifted his head again, and started to readjust her clothes. She gave a small cry of disappointment, which he silenced with a finger to her lips.

'I'm as nervous as a schoolboy, Antonia. Me!'

Is that why he's brought me to the brink and no further? She marvelled at his self-control, his command of the situation when it would have been so easy for him to carry on. She was reminded of how he'd behaved at the time of their accident, of his calmness in the face of crisis.

'Come. We should go in.' He took her firmly by the hand

and led her back into the villa. She trembled, though the night was warm.

His goodnight kiss that night was not designed to send her into a calm and dreamless sleep, and it did not. It was fierce and burning, a deliberate stoking of the smouldering embers of their desire. He parted her lips with his tongue almost roughly, searching the interior of her mouth with urgency, as if he wanted to know every nook and cranny of her being. The palm of one hand ran flat and hard down her spine, into the small of her back, and finally cupped her bottom, tilting her body up and against his, while with the other he reassured her breasts that they had not been forgotten.

'I want you, Antonia,' he rasped. 'Watch for me.' He left her to climb shakily up to her rooms. What did he mean, *watch for me*? And then she realised without any doubt what he meant. She remembered his lone figure standing far below her window, waiting, watching for her. He meant to wait for her again, and then what? She shivered with anticipation. Up in her rooms, she undressed with trembling fingers. In an effort to calm her nerves, she ran herself a warm bath into which she poured some soothing lavender oil. She lay for a while in the warm, fragrant water, looking at her own body with a new understanding. She realised that by the morning it would have gone through a change from which there was no turning back.

She traced the lines of her figure with her eyes, from the firm, high breasts, come alive since Lorenzo's touch; the slim waist by which he held her so often; and just below the line where her light golden tan was interrupted, the protective soft dark curls. Looking at her legs, Antonia knew she did not have the fashionable colt-like thinness of the elegant Swiss girl she had apparently supplanted, but it did not matter anymore. She realised that hers were beautiful legs, kept in shape by her habit of regular long walks, with firm calves and slender ankles.

'I am beautiful,' she told herself. 'He has brought out what was always there.'

She washed herself carefully and wrapped herself in one of the villa's warm, thick bath towels. After drying herself thoroughly, she took a clean nightdress of a fine cotton lawn from the old chest of drawers. Confused thoughts of virgin sacrifices placating the ancient gods of the surrounding mountains flitted through her mind. After parting the curtains of the net around her bed, she lay down on top of the sheets. It was a warm, sultry night, so she needed no other covering. Presently, from sheer emotional exhaustion, she began to doze fitfully.

She awoke in darkness, not knowing what it was that had stirred her from her sleep. Then she heard the sound again, this time consciously. The hoot of an owl in the still night, close to the villa. And then again, insistently, as she rubbed the sleep from her eyes. She checked the time on her phone – it was about half past midnight. *Watch for me*, he had said, the owl who watches by night. Antonia sat up suddenly, now completely awake. She slid off the bed, parted the mosquito net, and hurried to the window. It was open, and she eased back the creaking shutters. There he was, clearly visible in the moonlight, just as she had seen him on that earlier occasion. He was waiting for her, and his fierce whisper came up to her on the still air.

'*Che bella che sei!* How beautiful you are! Wait for me, my angel!' With those parting words he disappeared quickly from her view, running swiftly and lightly into the house.

Antonia sank into a chair, her heart thumping. Fear was mixed with anticipation. Was she doing the right thing? Who could advise her? *Silly, only you and he can decide if this is right. And whatever happens, I might never have the chance of such happiness ever again. I'll treasure forever the joy of being in his arms.*

She heard his tread upon the stairs, then his gentle tap on the door, and rushed to meet him. Lorenzo stood smiling softly, his eyes liquid and black with desire. He was holding an old-fashioned oil lamp. With his free arm he gathered her close against his naked chest.

'Oh my darling Antonia,' he murmured against her ear, 'I've come for you. Come with me now.'

Never before had she obeyed a command so willingly. Silently she slipped her hand into his and he led her downstairs to the villa's finest chambers on the floor below.

She moved as if in a dream, seeing the villa with fresh eyes in the flickering light of the oil lamp. As they moved across the marble floor of the first-floor corridor, the countess's antique furniture cast long shadows. A bronze figurine of a horse loomed up in the gloom, seeming larger than it really was in that ethereal light. The ancient Quattromani family portraits that lined the corridor appeared to move in and out of the shadows and take on a liveliness that their solemn features lacked in the daytime.

Presently Lorenzo opened one of the double doors of one of the prettiest rooms in the house, a delightful rococo bedchamber that could have graced Marie Antoinette's palace at Versailles. The bed itself was a magnificent four-poster, made intimate by the delicate embroidery of its curtains. In keeping with the gentle character of the room, with its faded sprigged wallpaper and ornaments of Dresden china, the only lighting came from a subdued lamp placed on a marble-topped bedside table.. But it was at the sight of the bed itself that Antonia's heart began to beat faster. The covers were turned back to reveal crisp white linen sheets, and a tumbling of lace-embroidered pillows.

'Lorenzo, it's beautiful!' she whispered.

'So are you,' he murmured, gently easing away her hair to kiss the nape of her neck. Then after he'd snuffed the lamp he carried and put it down, he took her shoulders and turned her to face him.

'My darling, I want this to be perfect for you – for both of us. I want you to want this for the rest of your life. I love you. You are my angel come down from heaven,' he told her, and with the tip of his finger below her chin he raised her face up to look at him.

'Thank you for coming to the window like that,' he continued. 'I had to see you again like that before I came for you, see you as I'd seen you in the moment I realised I'd fallen in love with you. I want to marry you, as soon as we can. Tonight, I want to show you what it could be like … I want …' his voice dropped to a pleading whisper, 'to make you want me forever.'

He led her to the bed and sat her tenderly back against the pillows.

She mutely obeyed him, watching him with parted lips as he stood back from her, never taking his eyes from her face, and started to unbuckle his leather belt. Antonia felt her blood pounding in her temples. The buckle of the belt hit the marble floor with a crack that resounded in that silent night like a gunshot, but Antonia did not have time to dwell on the sound. Lorenzo bent over her, his lips brushing her forehead, the tip of her upturned nose, her mouth.

'Touch me, my darling,' he urged her in a fierce whisper. Her hands had been itching to do just that. They stole up to his chest to stroke those silky hairs, her nails catching on his nipples, which stiffened in response as his tongue gently, familiarly, sought the inside of her mouth. Antonia felt all her fears evaporate as she surrendered back onto the pillows, his body following hers. Then she felt the power of his weight against her as she had that day on the hillside, overpowering her, dominating her every sense, but never crushing her. Slowly, he began to move against her body in an instinctive rhythm, and just as instinctively, her hands encircled him, the tips of her fingers exploring with delight the taut muscles of his back, insinuating themselves under the waistband of his light trousers.

Then with a soft moan he tore his mouth from hers, propped himself on one elbow and gazed down at her. 'I'm sorry, my darling, I'm rushing this,' he whispered. 'I'm forgetting that we've got the rest of our lives.' He caught the flicker of disappointment in Antonia's upturned face and laughed softly.

'Don't misunderstand me,' he reassured her, and affirmed his words with a rapid kiss. 'Tonight there will be no turning back.' He kissed her again, this time on her neck. He raised his head once more as he added, 'What I mean is that we will do this again,' his tongue flicked against her earlobe, 'and again,' this time his lips were at the neck of her nightdress, 'and again,' and he buried his face against her breasts, while her hands wound into his hair. When he spoke again his voice was ragged with desire. 'Let me see you, my darling.'

Antonia's face burned, but she raised herself up obediently and leaned forward, letting her hair fall loose about her, and in a deft movement pulled the nightdress quickly over her head. Then she lay back, naked against the lace pillows. What joy it gave her to watch his face, to follow his gaze as it raked hungrily over her. Her nipples hardened, her knees shifted almost imperceptibly apart. His probing hands, his expert fingers encouraged them further. She clung to him, drawing him against her, her hands fluttering ineffectually against the fastening of his trousers. With reluctance he drew away from her, though his focus stayed on her where she lay waiting for him. He stood by the side of the bed, turning his body slightly away from her as he slid his last remaining clothes from his narrow hips. He caught at the sheet to cover himself before he turned round to face her fully again. She reached out to him.

'No, no, let me see you too.'

He let the sheet fall.

'Antonia, I love you. He lay beside her and now his mouth strayed over her. At each point where his lips touched her satin skin her body seemed to come alive as never before. She felt with wonder the pressure of his erection where it touched her body, as if it had a warm life all of its own. His mouth and tongue travelled all over her, alternately kissing, teasing her flesh, while sometimes he muttered soft terms of endearment, *amore mio, tesoro*. Finally his lips took possession of her most secret places and her back arched with an ecstasy she could never have believed herself capable of reaching. Just as she thought she would die of this exquisite pleasure, she felt his mouth leave her, his body arch above hers, and she saw him looking down on her, his face almost distorted in the white heat of his desire.

'I want you,' he gasped out. 'I want you now and always.'

'Yes,' she breathed. 'Oh yes, Lorenzo, but—'

'I know. Look away just for a moment,' he said, looking boyish. She obeyed, as he reached for his trousers, pulling something from a pocket. There was a tearing sound, a snap, and then he covered her body with his, and her eyes, now looking up into his, closed with pain as finally he entered her. Tears of joy sprang to her eyes, and she clung, sobbing gently, to the man who was now her lover.

In the delicious rest that came after his possession of her, Lorenzo gently stroked her cheek and kissed away her tears. 'I hope I didn't disappoint you,' he murmured.

'You know you didn't.' She smiled up at him. He bent his head and teased her mouth gently with his. She felt his body stirring again against hers.

'Again?' she whispered tremulously, her arms stealing about his neck. She was amazed at her own audacity. 'Yes … yes,' he answered. 'Whenever you want me. You know I want you …' A moment later, he entered her once more.

'Marry me,' he groaned into her hair as his passion reached its height. In answer she pulled his head up until his face was above hers.

'Yes, Lorenzo, you know it's yes,' she cried.

A smile flooded his features before he threw his head back and with a shuddering groan thrust once more deep inside her before he sank, panting, onto her breasts.

His head was still cradled in her sleeping arms when the pale light of dawn began to filter through the shutters.

Chapter Nine

The following days were the happiest of Antonia's life, not least because Laura Quattromani gave them her blessing on their future marriage. Antonia reassured the countess that the work on the Quattromani archive would not be abandoned so close to the finish, and that whatever happened, she would not be whisked off to Gavedo for good. The wedding was planned for six months' time. She hated to leave a job incomplete, and besides, as she explained to an impatient Lorenzo, she needed to get used to the idea of marrying him, convinced though she was that she had made the right decision. Certainly his lovemaking, either in the pretty rococo bedroom of their first night together or when he joined her under the mosquito net in her own room, regularly helped to reassure her.

There was only one creeping doubt in Antonia's mind, but it refused to go away. Six weeks had come and gone, six weeks in which Lorenzo had come into her life and captured her body and soul. July had given way to sultry August. It was time that he went back to Gavedo to take care of the estate there, while she should be spending all hours working on the archive to finish her cataloguing. Antonia knew she would miss Lorenzo terribly, but none of this was what worried her.

Giselle Landsdorf would be back in Europe by now, Antonia knew, but there had been no news of her. Yet.

More than ever the countess had taken Antonia under her wing, just like an old mother hen.

'You're going to be a Quattromani soon,' she remarked cheerfully, 'though these days you don't get to change your surname, you know. We're liberated in Italy. But all in good time, you'll doubtless be the mother of Quattromanis. It's only right that you should get to know all the family skeletons. They'll be yours too soon enough.' And so the old lady proceeded to tell Antonia all the Quattromani folklore, stories of their exploits through the centuries. Antonia quickly realised that what the family members had recorded about themselves in their papers was only some small part of the whole story.

'Of course, the earliest members of the family were not very cultured people, quite the opposite in fact,' explained the countess. 'The thirteenth-century Quattromanis were *condottieri*, soldiers of fortune. Hired thugs, in other words. Not men of principle at all,' she continued with obvious relish. 'Our great Tuscany in those days was really a collection of city states, self-governed towns. Might was always the ruler. The Quattromanis made their money and acquired their lands by being in the pay of the right petty tyrant at the right time. If one ruler was going to war with another, and the Quattromani mercenaries thought they were backing the losing side, well, they'd start secret negotiations with their employer's enemies and make the switch – for the right price of course – at the time calculated to do the most damage. These mercenaries were running a business, you see, and as in business they had to take calculated risks and maximise the return on their assets. The fewer men a mercenary leader lost in battle the better. Soldiers were expensive to train, and experienced men were hard to replace. A mercenary certainly didn't encourage fighting to the death or other useless heroics out of misplaced loyalty to his employer. That would mean depreciating his investments. So he'd move over to what he saw as the safer bet. Of course, in later years, the men of the family got a bit more subtle about adding to their fortunes. They married rich heiresses instead. We Quattromanis have always been astute in business,' finished the old lady, laughing. 'Now are you still quite sure you want to join us?'

'I love him,' murmured Antonia, her head still full of the clash of steel and the groans of dying men. This beautiful landscape had certainly seen its dark days, right up to the rattle of bullets against the wall of the church at Gavedo.

'I know you do,' said the countess gently, 'and believe me, I'm so glad. You've transformed him. Either that or you've released the real Lorenzo, who was hidden. The one

I never knew existed. I had dismissed Lorenzo, you know. All I could see in him was my cruel brother when he was a young man. Now I see that sons are not always like their fathers.' The old lady broke off, wrapped up in the silence of her own memories.

'I saw those graves,' whispered Antonia. 'People had left flowers.'

The countess's gaze seemed fixed on the distance, on the mountains on the horizon visible through the tall windows of the library, but Antonia sensed that the old lady did not even see them. What she was staring at were her own memories.

'And to think that I have never had the courage to go to that terrible place.' A tear slid out of the old lady's eye but she seemed not to notice it. Suddenly she collected herself, and turning to face Antonia again asked her in a stronger voice, 'But how did you know? Lorenzo must have taken you.'

'He did,' Antonia answered gently.

The countess sighed and said half to herself, 'Yes, yes, I have misjudged the boy.'

Antonia went about the villa now with fresh eyes and with fresh enthusiasm for her work. She went again to look more closely at the Quattromani portraits that lined the corridor where the pretty rococo bedroom was. She was struck more and more by the startling resemblance of these long-dead faces to the living man who was her lover.

Here was the strong, determined chin, softer in the female portraits, though the Quattromani ladies certainly did not lack strength of character. Here was the Roman nose, there were the arched eyebrows, the high cheekbones. Above all, his startling slate-grey eyes stared back at her from above starched lace collars, suits of armour or the rich velvet of the age of Byron. Standing in front of the portrait of a Quattromani from the nineteenth century, a distinguished politician who had served in the first government of the newly-unified Italy, Antonia felt the arms of his descendant steal around her waist, the warmth of his breath on her cheek, and then a furtive kiss on her neck.

'I wonder what the senator would have to say about what goes on along this corridor,' he murmured throatily against her ear.

Antonia laughed, wriggling round in his arms to kiss the living man on his smiling mouth. 'Listen, my love,' he said. 'I've persuaded Aunt to spare you for a couple of days. Would you come to Gavedo with me? I need to see the estate manager and catch up on business, and besides, I want to show you off this time. I'd like you to meet all the vineyard's employees, since you'll be seeing much more of them ... and I promise to drive carefully.' Antonia hugged him still closer.

'I'd love to,' she said, 'but only on condition I get a better look at you in that swimming pool.' Then she continued in a more serious tone, 'And I'm not worried about your driving. That accident wasn't anybody's fault. In fact, if it hadn't been for your presence of mind, the unthinkable could have happened. In a way, it's brought us closer together.' She shivered for a moment in his arms.

'Dear Antonia, I love your way of looking at the world. I love your trust in me, and I'm never going to let you down. So Gavedo it is. Tomorrow morning, then?'

The gates of the Gavedo estates swung noiselessly open, and the Mercedes glided through.

'I should really have carried you through the gates, not driven you through,' laughed Lorenzo. 'This is to be your home, after all.'

Antonia was at a loss for words. The wonder of her situation took her breath away. 'Somebody pinch me,' she muttered. 'I thought this only happened in fairy tales.'

'You'll get used to it,' he reassured her comfortably, as if he were talking about something as commonplace as new wallpaper.

'Oh Lorenzo, I hope I never get used to it. I want all this' – she waved her arm at the passing landscape – 'to always be a wonder to me. And not just this place, but us as well.'

Instead of answering her, Lorenzo reached over and took her hand. Then, round a bend in the drive, the sturdy figure of a man in his forties came into view, wearing the simple clothes and tough boots of someone who has always worked on the land. Lorenzo slowed the big car to a halt. 'Well, that's lucky. We've met up with my estate manager already. Let me introduce you.'

Lorenzo jumped out of the car and shook the man's hand warmly. The estate manager immediately began talking about the affairs of the estate, and Lorenzo had to interrupt him to introduce Antonia, who by this time was standing shyly by the car.

'Paolo, let me introduce Antonia, my future wife,' he announced proudly.

Antonia could not fail to notice the look of alarm and concern which flickered over Paolo's weather-beaten features, and saw that Lorenzo did not miss it either. Always polite, however, the man shook Antonia's hand, bowed slightly and formally, before turning suddenly to his employer and blurting out, 'I – congratulations – I'm sorry … there's a visitor at the house. I didn't know, we let her in …'

Antonia was poised for a moment on the brink of anguish. Perhaps she had misunderstood the man? But no, his words were unmistakable, and reinforced by his obviously awkward and embarrassed behaviour. She had no doubt either about who the visitor was. Antonia felt as if an icy hand were gripping her heart, and for a moment she found it hard to breathe. Lorenzo had gone pale beneath his tan and his mouth was set in a hard, angry line. Without a word, just a nod of thanks, he clapped his hand twice on Paolo's shoulder as if to reassure him that none of this was his fault and steered a speechless Antonia back to the car.

He sat for a few moments behind the wheel without

starting the engine, his face set hard in a mask of anger. Finally he drew a ragged breath, and with his eyes still fixed ahead, he said, 'I'm sorry, Antonia. I don't know what Giselle can hope to achieve by this performance. I don't blame the estate staff for letting her in. They were none the wiser.'

He turned to face her and Antonia started with surprise at the look of pleading in his eyes.

'I hate to ask you this,' he continued, 'but please come with me. Once she sees us together, she'll have to realise I meant what I said when I told her we were over. I would have preferred to spare you this unpleasantness, but her extreme behaviour needs an extreme remedy. Lying in wait for me! It's so strange, I really didn't think it was her style.'

In reply, Antonia took his hand in both of hers and kissed it lightly.

'Of course I'll come with you,' she whispered, afraid to speak louder in case he heard the trembling in her voice.

'Oh my dear girl,' he murmured with gratitude. Then he started the car, much to Antonia's relief. The sooner this was over with the better. The sound of the engine disguised the frantic beating of her heart. They headed off towards the ruined castle and Lorenzo's home.

The mud-splattered, sleek white sports car with the Zurich number plate was parked at an angle in front of the farmhouse, in such a way that there was no space for anyone else, so Lorenzo stopped the Mercedes some distance away, hurrying round the car to help out a shaking Antonia. He held her hand grimly, as though he never ever meant to let it go, and they walked slowly towards the house.

As they approached, the Swiss girl appeared in the doorway, dressed simply but expensively and elegantly as always, in tight white cotton trousers, a fine grey silk shirt and Gucci loafers. Her pale blond hair fell around her beautiful, cold face, which was wearing its customary smirk. She leaned casually against the door frame, as if she owned the place, thought Antonia with a sudden spurt of anger. Then her heart seemed to miss a beat as she caught the undisguised malice – and triumph – in Giselle's cold eyes. The Swiss girl was the first to speak.

'Very pretty, I'm sure. Really, Lorenzo, I wouldn't have minded half so much had your little fling been with someone beautiful, but that little nobody.'

Antonia could not help but recoil at the venom in Giselle's words, but Lorenzo's response was quick and curt. 'Leave now, before my staff throw you off the estate as a trespasser. And don't come back. You'll get no more chances to insult my future wife like that ever again.'

Giselle did not move. Antonia thought her coolness was astounding. The woman laughed for a moment, a brittle, joyless sound. Then with a strange proprietary gesture she stroked one slim hand twice across the gentle incline of her stomach.

'Your future wife?' she sneered. 'And what about

your future heir? Thoroughbreds should breed with thoroughbreds, not weaken their pedigree by mating with some beast of burden.'

Lorenzo was now white with anger, and it was lucky that Antonia had the presence of mind to restrain him. There was a terrible threat in the Swiss girl's words that Lorenzo still did not seem to understand. When Giselle spoke again, her meaning was crystal clear, and Antonia felt her whole world, her hopes, her dreams, come crashing around her ears.

'Strike me, would you?' taunted Giselle. 'Strike me and your unborn child?'

The effect of these words on Lorenzo was electrifying. He stopped dead, as if he had been shot and was about to collapse to the ground. His lips were white and bloodless, his eyes staring with shock. His former lover drew herself up, her lip curling. She had played her trump card. This was her moment of triumph. She had won, and all three of them knew it.

'But you were on the pill,' Lorenzo eventually said.

'I was, wasn't I? Well, I came off it.'

What seemed like a long silence was finally broken by Antonia's low cry of pain, the cry of a wounded animal. She tore her hand away from Lorenzo's and turned and ran down the path, blinded by her tears, staggering and falling against stones, picking herself up again and running on. She was unaware of the blood on her knees and on her grazed hands, only conscious of her tears, the tears that come when all hope is crushed. She found herself at last by the abandoned castle. The forlorn appearance of the ruin seemed to symbolise everything she felt in that moment. She threw herself against the rough wall, clinging to it for support, her nails breaking and splintering as she struck her hands repeatedly against the masonry, her body wracked by sobs. Then suddenly she felt strong arms about her, supporting her, and heard Lorenzo's frantic voice pleading with her.

'Antonia, Antonia, don't leave me. Don't ever leave me. She tricked me, that fiend. I don't know how, heaven knows, she always convinced me that she was so careful, she told me she was taking care of everything. Antonia, you must believe me, Giselle wants my money. That, and some prestige, was all she ever wanted from me. To stoop so low to get it ...' he went on in a distracted voice. 'Well, she can have as much money as she wants, I would never run away from my responsibilities. Oh Antonia, for pity's sake, don't stop loving me.'

Random words filtered through to Antonia's shocked and confused brain. But she recovered enough strength of mind to push away his hands, and she leaned back a little against the castle's ancient wall as if it gave her strength for what she was about to say.

'Love you?' she cried. 'I do love you and always will. I couldn't stop myself if I tried. You might as well ask me to stop breathing as to do that. Even this cannot change that.'

'Oh Antonia,' he cried, as he tried to take her in his arms again.

'No,' she shouted, putting up both hands in a sharp gesture of refusal. 'Lorenzo, I will love you for as long as I live, but I will not marry you.' She could see his despair but she carried on. 'Don't you see, Lorenzo, money is the easy part? Of course, you must support your child, give him or her the best, but that's never going to be enough. A child needs a father when he speaks his first words, when he wakes up from a nightmare, when he goes to school for the first time. Money can't buy a father's presence. Believe me, I know. My mother toiled to keep herself and me going, all those miserable part-time, badly paid jobs she did to make sure she'd always be at home when I came in from school, because no one else was. All that sewing she took in for women who were too idle or too proud to even sew on buttons. Those cleaning jobs that ruined her hands. Money was always a problem for us, but had my father been there, had he given her some care, some relief and affection in her loneliness and mine, how different our lives might have been. But he'd have needed to have been a different man for that. All I wanted was to be like other children, to have both Mum and Dad there on school parent nights. Lorenzo, I cannot possibly marry you. I'd be stealing you from someone who needs you more. Your innocent child.'

Lorenzo was as cowed as a whipped dog, but he answered her with desperate pleading in his voice. 'Antonia, this child would never be like other children, whatever I did. Can you honestly see Giselle as a mother? As soon as she's given birth, she'll hand the baby over to hired help, just like what happened to me. Her concern won't be with feeding him, changing him, giving him the love he needs, it'll be with getting her figure back as soon as possible. The moment she can, she'll have him packed off to boarding school out of her way, like hundreds of other rich, lonely and, yes, abandoned children. He'll cry into strange pillows when he's five years old, just like I did.'

'All the more reason for you to be with him,' countered Antonia, her eyes brimming with tears at the thought of what might be in store for this poor child.

'Don't do this to me,' he pleaded. 'Don't make me miserable for the rest of my life. Antonia, don't make me hate this innocent child.'

'You won't hate him,' she murmured softly through her tears, as she relented and took his hands in hers. 'If you love me, love this baby for me. You must, Lorenzo.'

'I can't let you go, Antonia. You're the best thing that ever happened to me,' he murmured brokenly, but she could tell from his tone that he had already accepted that it was the end.

'And you to me, Lorenzo, believe me. But now you must make this child the best thing in your life. You know we have no choice. Now, call Luigi,' she added, her voice trembling. 'I will go back to the villa alone. I must.'

'No!' exclaimed Lorenzo. 'You can't leave me.'

'Oh my darling, I never could,' she cried, her tears falling afresh. 'I will always be with you, but only here in my heart. I will never stop loving you. We will always be lovers, you and I, though you will never hold me in your arms again. Please, don't make this any worse. I'll call Luigi ...'

'No, I'll do it. And I'll speak to my aunt. This is all my fault, not yours. And because of it I'm going to lose the only thing that has been good and true in my entire life.' He tore himself away, tears shimmering in his eyes, and stumbled back up the path to the house.

Ten minutes later he returned and took her in his arms. 'Holding you like this,' he said, 'will have to last me a lifetime.' His cheek against hers, he said, 'Luigi will be here soon. And he's bringing my aunt. It'll be the first time she's set foot here in decades ... I wish she had come for any reason but this. I started blurting out the whole story to Luigi ... and then he said he was going to speak to her. I could hear the catch in his voice, poor man. He is so fond of you, you know, him and Elena. My aunt came on the line, and she was crying, but said nothing would stop her coming.'

And so Laura Quattromani had come, to be there in Antonia's hour of need, and Lorenzo's. Slowly the two of them got to their feet, still holding hands.

Laura Quattromani embraced her nephew first, then holding his face between her old hands, murmured in Italian,

'My poor boy, that it all must end this way.'

Then she took Antonia in her comforting arms. 'My poor girl, the daughter I never had. Come home.' Supporting each other, for the old lady still did not walk too well and Antonia was numb with shock, they stumbled towards Luigi's car.

Once inside she cried, 'I don't know how to bear this,' and hid her face in the countess's shoulder, sobbing while her heart broke. She was barely conscious of the car starting to move, but when she came to her senses and realised they were going away, she twisted round wildly to see Lorenzo through the back window. He was running desperately after the little car, waving and shouting her name, but his tall figure inexorably receded on the bumpy road, and though she kept him in her sights until her eyes stung from not blinking, she eventually could see him no more.

Sitting at the rough-hewn table in the entrance hall of Lorenzo's home, Giselle shut her eyes and dragged deeply on a menthol cigarette. A good day's work, she thought. Then suddenly her peace was shattered, the cigarette torn from her lips, the ashtray smashing to pieces on the tiled floor.

'What do you think you're doing?' shouted Lorenzo hoarsely. 'You care so little for our child?'

'Forgive me, my darling. It was my first in ages, really. And you must admit, it's been such a stressful day,' she murmured. 'But now that you're back, everything will be just fine!' Getting to her feet, she attempted to put her hands around Lorenzo's neck. He recoiled as though the touch of her fingers burned his skin. He prised her hands away and took several steps back.

'No, it won't be just fine,' he spat out. 'Understand one thing. I'm here because of our child, and only because of our child, because I will care for him even if you don't. The woman I love made me promise her that. Now hear this, I'll stay with you, I'll take care of you both. But Antonia should have been my wife, and I will always think of her in that way. Happy, now?'

Chapter Ten

'England,' murmured Antonia, looking out on a grey, drizzly September day as the flight from Pisa touched down at London's Gatwick airport. She threaded her way through the long corridors of Arrivals, feeling as if she had lived a lifetime in the last few weeks, and tried hard not to remember how she'd felt as she'd set out from this same airport. A new life, a new beginning – smashed to pieces. *Perhaps I'm never meant to find happiness. The most I can hope for is to survive.*

In the Arrivals hall, Antonia anxiously scanned the faces of the people meeting the Pisa flight, searching for Jane's friendly face. The flight had seemed mainly to consist of people returning from their longed-for Tuscan holidays, warmed body and soul by the gentle late summer sun, the beautiful landscape, the smoothness of the wine and the kindness of the people. She'd seen some honeymoon couples on the plane, clearly still intoxicated by the novelty of married life and their discovery of each other. Antonia was grateful she had not been sitting next to any of them.

They'll always remember Italy as that lovely welcoming country where everyone congratulated them and wished them happiness. They wouldn't want me dampening their joy.

Pushing her two battered suitcases onto an airport trolley, Antonia finally caught sight of her friend.

'Oh, Antonia!' Jane exclaimed, and Antonia saw the shock in her face. The two girls hugged, then Jane said, 'Is this all you have?'

'That's right. All of my life is in those bags, It's just them and me now.'

'You've got thinner,' said Jane, stroking her cheek. 'Your clothes are hanging off you. I hate that sadness in your eyes.'

'I think even my hair has forgotten to curl,' sniffed Antonia.

'No, you're as beautiful as ever. And now you're going to take on London.'

'Oh don't, Jane.'

'I'm being clumsy, I'm sorry.'

'Don't say that,' Antonia cried. 'I can't tell you how glad I am to see you.'

'I'll always be here for you, you know that. Not sure about my car, mind. I was in my usual mad rush to get here and so I forgot to make a note of exactly where I left it in the car park.'

Antonia's spirits lifted in spite of herself as for fifteen minutes or so they raced up and down with the baggage trolley looking for the car, laughing at Jane's scatter-brained parking. When finally they were leaving the airport, Jane turned to her friend and said simply, 'I'm listening, whenever, if ever, you want to talk.'

'Thank you, Jane, I'm so grateful for that, and I will. Just now, though, I'm so confused I don't know where to turn, but I'll have to put all my energy into something practical. I have to find a job, somewhere to live ...'

Somewhere to live. As she said those words, a vision swam across Antonia's eyes of an abandoned castle, ruined but still standing proud above rows of flourishing vines, a castle that cried out to be cared for, to be restored to its former glory. She no longer saw the modern buildings of the airport terminal, the interlocking roads around them busy with screaming traffic coming and going, or the faceless hotels catering for travellers who wanted to be anywhere but in them. Her vision was blurred with tears.

'Antonia,' Jane said softly, and Antonia could hear the compassion in her voice. 'You've got so much kindness, so much love in your heart, so much to give. One day, when you least expect it, you'll find someone worthy of your love.'

'Oh, but I have,' answered Antonia, in a surprisingly strong voice, despite the tears. 'He was worthy of me. He loved me – he loves me now. But fate was against us. Nothing else could ever come close to what we had.'

Jane patted Antonia's arm briefly. Antonia felt the reassurance of her friend's touch, grateful that Jane didn't try to slather her in platitudes of optimism or promises that the pain would pass and she would love again. It was too early to hear them, and Antonia, despite her misery, was thankful for her friend's restraint.

'This man,' Jane murmured, 'must have been quite exceptional.'

'Anyway,' Antonia went on, 'I've got to live. I'll email Arthur Bennett this evening, see what advice he can give me about a job. I'll take anything in the meantime so I can get by. Cutbacks in libraries mean the work I'm qualified for is going to be really hard to find. I'm determined not to take advantage of your hospitality and kindness for any longer than is necessary.'

'Antonia, you know it's always a real pleasure for us to see you. There's absolutely no rush. Make sure you find the right job, the right place to live before you pack up and move on. You need some stability in your life,' Jane said shrewdly. 'Your inner strength will pull you through,' she added, 'but I know that doesn't make the pain you must be going through now any easier.'

Bit by bit over the next few days, in the comfort and security of Jane and Simon's home, Antonia spilled out the whole sad story. It affected her two friends deeply, and Simon's sympathy went out in particular to Lorenzo, caught in a terrible trap that he had unwittingly set for himself.

'Imagine how that man must be feeling,' he murmured one evening as they sat together watching the telly. 'To have to stay by the side of a woman he can only despise for the trick she has played on him, to watch as his child grows inside her and is born to her when he must all the time be imagining you, Antonia, in her place. It's so cruel to him, to everybody. If I were him, I think I'd go mad. Imagine, if I found myself tied to someone else instead of you!' He hugged his wife close to himself with relief. Antonia smiled a small smile – her friends had so much love, but it tore at her inside to know what she'd lost.

Antonia threw all her energies into finding herself a job, and with it, a new life. Before too long, with Arthur Bennett's help, she found work. It was about as different as it could have been from the job in the little library in the sleepy Somerset town where he and she had worked together. This job was at the other end of the country, in an industrial town in County Durham, a town that had been ravaged by the closure of the steelworks that had sustained it for decades and by the disappearance, one by one, of the surrounding coal-pits. However, with new industry and start-ups encouraged, what Antonia found there was not all gloom and doom, but a friendly and welcoming people, strong in the face of adversity and determined to fight back for a better life.

Valerie Clark was the chief librarian, and Antonia was to be her second-in-command. They took to each other as soon as they met. They weren't running just one library, but six small branches across quite a wide area, as well as a mobile service. All the other staff were committed and enthusiastic volunteers in desperate need of training. Valerie was blunt. 'Normally you'd have been in line for my role when I retire, but there are no guarantees it'll exist anymore. You're going to have to be pretty resilient. This is where I grew up, and I can tell you the people here have been through the mill. Libraries have to be a beacon, not just a place for a quiet read but also a centre for new learning, new discoveries, new lives.'

Antonia thought about all she'd gone through and all the people who were now relying on her to do a good job, and said, 'I'm what you want. Just keep me so busy I haven't time to think.'

Valerie laughed, 'Oh, I think we'll manage that, hinny.'

Antonia threw herself into getting to know her readers' needs and interests, just as she had in Somerset. Valerie voiced her approval that thanks to Antonia's energy and enthusiasm, the number of books issued from the library went up, and people who had never in their lives thought a library could be for them started to use it regularly. Antonia organised events for the children, published a local events guide, and set up an exhibition area for the local art club.

'You know, I don't think I've ever been so busy in my life before,' she remarked to Valerie one evening as they were locking up the library after another whirlwind of a day.

'Well, so long as you're still enjoying yourself,' laughed her boss.

'Oh yes, the weeks have really hurtled by.'

'Weeks?' exclaimed Valerie. 'Don't you realise you've been here more than six months already?'

'Six months?' gasped Antonia. Six months it was, of course. The bleak winter was already giving way to spring, with snowdrops and crocuses starting to push their optimistic little heads through the frosty earth, and there was a promise in the air of forthcoming warmth. She had dedicated herself to her work, so much so that on occasion she found Valerie regarding her with a reproving air, and more than once her boss had said to her, 'You're exceptional, Antonia. I've never had a colleague like you, so hard working and dedicated. You really care about what you do, but mind you don't overdo it.'

It could have been Laura Quattromani speaking, thought Antonia with a wrench. Weeks or months or even years, it made no difference. The pain of loss would never go away. Working hard just helped to deaden the ache a little. She still felt as if she had physically lost some part of herself, and now she would have to find some way of compensating, of adapting to a different kind of life. There could never be any replacement for her lost love. But in spite of everything she regretted nothing. So many people go through life without ever experiencing real love. At least I will always have my memories of being in his arms.

Her memories were tinged with anger, too. Giselle Landsdorf, she knew, was one of those people who would never experience love in their lives, for the simple reason that she was not capable of giving it, except to herself. Antonia thought of the child Giselle and Lorenzo were going to bring into the world. Would that child ever experience his mother's love? Antonia had her doubts, and wept for that poor baby as well as for herself.

At night she dreamed of Lorenzo sometimes, and saw his face as if she had left him only yesterday. Once she dreamed she saw him standing in the entrance to the little chapel, and the air was heavy with the scent of lilies. She called out to him and tried to reach him, but though she ran up the path as fast as her feet would carry her, the chapel never got any nearer. He never seemed to hear her, though she saw him shade his eyes with his hand as he scanned the horizon, and heard him call her name.

Sometimes she knew she had dreamed of him though she remembered nothing about the dream, because she would wake in the darkness to find the pillow wet with tears.

Antonia thought of the tiny flat she rented near the library as her sanctuary, and she rapidly made it her own. Counting all the space in it, the bedroom, sitting room, galley kitchen and tiny bathroom, it was not even as big as the bedroom that Antonia had had at the countess's villa, but she was not in it all that often, because she had become fully involved in the life of the small town. Instead she would come back at night only to fall, exhausted but satisfied, into her little bed. She knew she had turned all the love and happiness she had been denied into making other people happy. The alternative, she understood, would have been to become bitter and spiteful at the world. She remembered her mother's example, always calm, always there for her, even in her last illness. Her mother had never allowed frustration and anger to get the better of her, and she was her mother's daughter.

Early in the spring, aware that her Italian language was slipping away from disuse, Antonia enrolled on an evening course at the local college. The teacher was a motherly lady from near Venice who had married an English serviceman. Antonia was relieved that Benedetta's accent was nothing like the Tuscan one she was used to, and that made it easier to pay attention to the lessons. Pleased with her progress, Benedetta passed on to Antonia the gossip magazines her sister sent her. Back in her little flat Antonia riffled through these, deciding which one to treat herself to first. Then what she saw made her sink to her knees in despair.

Game Over! screamed the headline on the cover, the English phrase standing out. Antonia looked to see which VIP couple was getting married and saw Lorenzo, as elegantly sleek as a 1930s film star and just as remote, and on his arm, Giselle looking haughty in duchesse satin. 'Lorenzo Quattromani, heir to the Quattromani estates in Tuscany, weds Lausanne native at the sumptuous Beau Rivage Palace on Lake Geneva … Phil Collins married here and the venue is a favourite with Keanu Reeves…' burbled the text. Her heart thumping and her fingers trembling, Antonia opened the magazine in search of the full article, and peered at the pictures. Lorenzo stood stiff-backed before a dark-suited official. Giselle smirked. There seemed to be hundreds of people there. She recognised some television stars, but the other glittering guests in their effortlessly elegant clothes, the women dripping with diamonds, she did not know.

His aunt isn't there. She felt a little fierce stab of unexpected pleasure. *She's loyal – to me.* Then another thought crossed her mind. *Is she all right?* She looked at the date of the magazine. It was months old. *I must email her.*

Antonia spent the night in tears. But in the morning, she made herself get up and look at the photographs again. Yes, the only person there who did not seem to be happy was Lorenzo himself. Even now her heart ached for him. *I love you too much to see you so sad.*

Valerie looked up in alarm when she saw Antonia coming into the staff room. 'Should you be here, Antonia? You're so pale.'

'I should definitely be here, Valerie. More than ever.'

Antonia filled up her occasional days off with helping on school trips. Many a hard-pressed school teacher was grateful for Antonia's help and boundless energy. She smiled when the children approached, and as she grew to know and love the country around her, she worked to pass on her enthusiasm to the children themselves. A year went by in a whirl. One crisp, sunny April day she went with a class of seven-year-olds to the lovely county town of Durham and watched the joy on their faces as they explored every corner of the ancient and beautiful city.

'Why are there two castles here?' one eager little boy asked Antonia.

'That's not a castle, that's a cathedral,' she corrected him, but she could understand his mistake. The Norman cathedral rose like a vast fortress above the lush banks of the River Wear, an imposing sight she and the children would surely never forget, especially once they had climbed up the many steps of the main tower to a stupendous view over the medieval city. The cathedral dwarfed the actual castle of Durham that stood near it. The little party saw many wonderful places that day, but one that was a particular success was the old city lock-up. The children peered in at the bars and heavy studded doors, their mouths open in silent fascination.

'That's where you'll all go the next time you're naughty!' their teacher told them jokingly. The children squealed with delighted terror, and Antonia exchanged a wink with the teacher.

A final high point to the day was the boat trip around the peninsula on which the old city was built. The children were not so boisterous now, lolling about dead tired on the seats. They were clearly worn out by cathedral steps and all they had seen that day, as well as by the fresh air they had gulped into their lungs.

'I'm so grateful to you, Antonia, and the children really love you. The whole school hopes you'll never go away,' the teacher told her with heartfelt thanks as they took the opportunity to have a well earned rest while the boat chugged gently along the river.

'Well, I've no plans to go anywhere,' Antonia replied a little sadly. 'Besides, I enjoy days like this, and I love my work. There are probably very few people who can really say that.'

'I'm so glad you feel that way,' said the teacher. 'But sometimes in my work I wonder if I'm fighting a losing battle. The world isn't such a safe place for children, and you wonder what awaits them when they grow up and leave school. What chances will there be for them, what will their horizons be?'

Antonia was once more before the ruined castle of Gavedo, not as she was on that last terrible occasion, but as she was when Lorenzo had taken her there the first time, the day she had glimpsed his lithe, naked body in the swimming pool, the day he had comforted her in the shell of the burned-out church. They peered into the abandoned and rotting rooms of what had once been a grand and dignified home, and she heard his voice again, as clear as a church bell sounding in an Italian valley. 'Who knows what ideas you might have?'

As if it was the most natural and obvious thing in the world, she replied, 'A centre for young people, of course.

A place where they can learn new skills, broaden their horizons ...'

The vision faded. Her school teacher friend was holding Antonia's shoulders, searching her face with a concerned expression.

'Antonia, are you all right? You look so pale, and you were off in another world. We've tired you out today, me and the children. It's not fair of us, I'm so sorry.'

Antonia brushed a hand across her forehead, as if to brush away the cobwebs of her dreams.

'No, I'm fine, honestly. Nothing a good night's sleep won't cure. The children's enthusiasm is infectious, but perhaps I haven't always got the energy to keep up with them.'

'For a moment you seemed to be miles away,' said the teacher kindly, 'but you still carried on our conversation, wherever it was you'd gone to. You were murmuring something about a centre for young people, a way of broadening their horizons.'

'Oh well, that's good news. At least I wasn't talking complete nonsense,' laughed Antonia, relieved she hadn't given more away. 'A centre for young people, I said, did I? Well now, that might just be an idea ...'

'An early night for you, young lady,' the teacher said, pretending to scold her. 'That's quite enough thinking about other people for one day.' It certainly was, thought Antonia. The clarity of her vision had quite alarmed her. Had all the emotional stress and strain actually unbalanced her?

Antonia became more and more settled in her new life, outwardly at least. She could see the months and years mapped out before her, perhaps not the life she had imagined for herself, but certainly a worthwhile way of living. Laura Quattromani answered her restrained email, in which she'd pretended that she only wanted to know if the old lady was keeping well, and hoped she was having no more falls. Antonia thought about what Laura's email said for a long time, but deliberately damped down the little flicker of hope it gave her.

'Two librarians from the state archive in Florence have been to see me,' wrote Laura.

They were extremely impressed by the catalogue of the Quattromani papers that you compiled, and they are putting it online with a link through their own site so that scholars will know of the existence of the archive and can come and study Gianluca's writings. They are also talking about scanning some items so that they can be instantly available on the internet. So I expect to see many more visitors in future, though I do wish you were one of them. They propose putting on an exhibition in Florence about our Gianluca, which would then go on to the British Library in London and to the Library of Congress in Washington. They want you to be involved. I know that coming back here is quite possibly the last thing you want to do and I will understand if you say no, but do think about it. The only comfort I can give you, if it is comfort at all, is that you won't see my nephew. From what little I know of his doings, he knows he has made the wrong choice. I am an old woman, and I never found anyone who would have had enough patience to be married to me, but though I was brought up always to do the right thing sometimes that right thing can be completely wrongheaded.

I'm sorry, I am digressing and I really only wanted to ask you about Gianluca and was trying not to rake up anything that would cause you pain, though I am still so angry at how things turned out. Please send me your news, dear Antonia. I miss you very much, and Luigi and Elena also send their love.

Antonia shared some of the contents of the email with Valerie.

'You must go, Antonia! I'll see if I can get you the time off, maybe a combination of holiday time and some unpaid leave if you can manage that. This is an unmissable opportunity.'

'I'm not sure, Valerie.'

Antonia's boss looked at her shrewdly. 'More happened in Italy than you've told me about, didn't it? Well, I'm not going to pester you about it, but I'm here if you want to talk. But don't let some man get in the way of the rest of your life, Antonia.'

That same week the landlord of her little rented flat decided to put it up for sale, but Antonia managed to turn this potential upheaval into an opportunity for both of them.

'I like it here, Mr Hudspeth,' she explained when he came round to give her notice. 'Would you consider selling to me?'

'Yes, of course. I just never considered you'd be wanting to stay in this town so long, a young lass like you with her life in front of her.'

'My life is here now,' she said, with a sad little smile. 'It's time I settled, put down some roots.'

'Well, if you're sure,' he replied. 'Of course I'd be glad to sell to you. And I'll knock the price down a bit. I'm not going to have the usual bother with lawyers that way, and I'll not need to be paying any fees to an estate agent. Plus the fact you've saved me a lot of aggravation. It can take a while to sell a place around here nowadays.'

'That's done, then,' said Antonia. 'I'll start my mortgage application straightaway.'

Antonia thought she knew all of her readers well, but she could not remember having seen this gentle old lady before. As the queue at the issue desk moved quickly forward, Antonia noticed out of the corner of her eye that the old lady was doing something very odd. She was asking each new person who joined the queue to go ahead of her. Indeed, she insisted on it. At that rate the old soul would never get served, thought Antonia. Really, it was taking courtesy a little too far. Why? Then it dawned on her. The old lady must be wanting to speak to her personally, and did not want to be interrupted while she did so. It was a busy lunchtime and the library staff took their breaks in turn, to ensure uninterrupted service. One of the assistants was due back in about five minutes in order to let Antonia away. At least the poor old soul was not going to have to wait too long.

'Lunchtime! Off you go, you workaholic!' called out Lauren, a young mother who volunteered in the library while her children read and played in the children's corner.

'Thanks, Lauren,' replied Antonia, not failing to notice the little look of panic in the elderly stranger's eyes, as if she was afraid of losing her opportunity to speak to Antonia at last. To encourage her, Antonia gave the old lady a friendly smile as she came out from behind the counter.

'I'm after talking to you, so I am,' explained the old lady.

Irish. Well, no surprise in that. There were plenty of elderly Irish people in this little town, people who had come over looking for work and who had settled near the pit and the steelworks. Their children had been born here, but now they were moving on in their turn, as opportunities that their parents had taken up were no longer there. But Antonia was convinced that she had never seen this particular old lady before. This was odd. The library was such a focal point in the town and an important part of life for so many elderly people.

The woman seemed particularly keen to talk to Antonia

out of earshot of the library counter, and she was happy to oblige her.

With one hand on her arm, the old lady explained in a conspiratorial whisper, "Tis a romance I'm after!'

'Oh, but that's no problem,' Antonia reassured her. 'We have a special display for romances. They're always very popular. Let me show you.'

'Ah, but you see my dear, it's a very particular romance I'm after, and I need your help to find it,' said the Irishwoman mysteriously.

'Tell me all about it, and I'll see what I can do,' said Antonia. She was a little puzzled, it was true, but the old lady was certainly harmless, and Antonia was always pleased to help. The old lady drew her to the nearest chairs, which happened to be in the children's corner. In order to sit down they had to step round a young father who was murmuring to a toddler in a pushchair, but he had his back to them and did not see them to move out the way. Other, bigger children milled around, talking excitedly or waving picture books in the air. The library was a popular place with parents and children alike, and it was a natural stopping place on the way home for the little ones who finished nursery school at lunchtime, so this was the busiest part of the day. It did not, however, seem to worry the old lady. In the midst of all this juvenile mayhem, she started to tell a puzzled Antonia all about the kind of romance she wanted to read.

'This romance I'm looking for, my dear, didn't end well,

so I thought I'd take it upon myself to change the ending,' the old lady began. Antonia was startled. *Oh dear, I'd thought she was perfectly alert, but perhaps the poor lady is a bit confused – though there can be no harm in her.* Antonia decided the best thing to do would be to listen to her patiently and politely.

'Now, you'll be thinking I'm a bit mad, surely,' twinkled the old lady mischievously. 'Sure and you'd be right! There's not a romance under the sun that doesn't have a happy ending, isn't that so?'

Antonia gulped. There was clearly nothing confused about her companion. Quite a mind-reader she was. All she could manage to stammer out in reply was, 'Y-yes, of course. That's what makes a romance a romance.' She could not help adding, 'But real life isn't always like that.'

'Just listen to you, you such a young soul and such an old head on your shoulders. Now will you humour an old lady and let her be telling you this story?'

Antonia was intrigued, and said so. Vague memories of tales she had heard of Irish storytellers came back. As a librarian she had been taught to take care of the written word, but not to forget the great verbal traditions on which so many stories were based. She was now genuinely curious to hear what the old lady had to tell her. She certainly looked ordinary enough, wearing a warm cardigan, a neatly pressed blouse, woollen skirt and sensible shoes. But the story she started to weave had a magical fascination which was anything but ordinary and Antonia listened spellbound as the old voice went on in its beautiful Irish lilt.

'Now, the heroine of this story must be beautiful, like all heroines in fairy stories, but this one is particularly beautiful because she is pure and good. Her skin is creamy like a freshly peeled apple, her eyes as blue as the sea on a summer's day, and her rich brown hair just won't be tamed. Something like yourself, in fact. Sure, she sounds like an Irish princess, but strange thing is, she's not Irish at all. Pity, that, but then I never wrote this story. She's not a princess either, but a poor orphan, or as good as.

'Now, this lovely girl leaves her home because there's little comfort for her there, and travels a long way to a warm and sunnier clime, and goes to live in a beautiful big house high up in the mountains. And because this is a romance, she must meet her hero there, a man as handsome as she is beautiful. Now, because she falls in love with him she thinks he's far better looking a fella than she is a pretty girl, but then that's the nature of love for you. Our hero can't be said to be perfect – but then what man is, and I'm not telling you any ordinary fairy tale. Since he's in love too by now he resolves to mend his ways. Now, what do you think of my story up to now? Have you the patience to hear an old woman out?'

'Oh yes, please go on,' begged Antonia, entranced at the novel way the old lady had of telling her tale. 'So why are you looking so sad, dear love you?' queried the old lady.

'You've been in love before and it didn't work out, I'd guess.'

'Oh, no, it's nothing. Just thoughts, that's all,' muttered Antonia, feeling a bit uncomfortable and wishing the old lady would continue telling her story.

'Ah now, I'd almost forgotten. There has to be a villain of the piece – or rather, in this case, a villainess. Do you remember that fairy tale about the Snow Queen?' asked the old lady.

'Well, yes, I think I do remember. My – my mother told me. The Snow Queen was very beautiful, but hard and cold, with a chip of ice for a heart,' murmured Antonia, recalling a distant memory from her happiest days of early childhood.

'Well now, that's what our heroine had to cope with, you see. There was this Snow Queen, so there was, who thought she had the young man all to herself, and had cast her spells on him, in a manner of speaking. It took our heroine, good and pure, to bring him to his senses, but the Snow Queen could not forgive either of them for foiling her plans. She had already suspected what might happen, and had started to plot!' finished the old lady in a dramatic stage whisper. Antonia glanced round quickly, but the children and parents milling about were much too concerned with their own activities to notice the old lady's mild eccentricity.

The storyteller now leaned forward and her voice dropped to a murmur. Antonia had to strain to hear her words above the din that surrounded them.

'She tricked him, you see. She wanted to make sure he

would never leave her. Her frozen heart was calculating and manipulative, but she knew his wasn't, and so she took advantage of this. She deliberately set out to play on his pity and his sense of duty, but her real triumph was bringing our poor heroine into the plot to support her dastardly plans. This is a modern tale, you see. The Snow Queen didn't cast any supernatural spells this time. She didn't need to.' The old lady paused, then her expression grew dark and disapproving.

'She trapped him with a child, you see. She didn't want a child, she didn't even really want the young man, but she was so spoiled and selfish she'd do anything to stop anyone else from getting him. That included allowing herself to get pregnant. And of course, our heroine insisted the young man leave her for the Snow Queen for the sake of the child.'

Antonia flushed deeply, and glanced wildly round. Was she dreaming? Was this some kind of horrible hallucination? Had the strain got too much for her, and just like that day on the boat with the school teacher, had she got confused between memories and reality? *Pull yourself together, get a grip!* Who was this old Irishwoman and how did she manage to touch such a nerve?

The old lady drew herself up for effect before she continued.

'Now, I suppose you think that's where the story ends. Not much of a romance, is it, with no happy ending? Well let me tell you what happens next.

'In the course of time a poor little baby boy was born. I call him poor not because he had no money, because he lacked for nothing that way. He was much poorer than that. His mother didn't love him. In fact, quite the opposite. She had thought the little boy was a sure way of catching our hero. She had succeeded in dragging him away from the girl he loved, but as far as the wicked woman was concerned the man might as well have been on the other side of the world. He adored his son, but though he and the little boy had each other, the two of them were the loneliest people in the universe ...' The old voice tailed off. Antonia summoned the courage to look up and meet the old lady's eyes. They were filled with tears.

'I looked after a lonely little boy once,' whispered the old lady. 'He had everything he could want, except the love of his mother and father. A child needs a father, Antonia, but he also needs a mother. Could you love this child, Antonia, even though he's not your own? Could you love him just as you love his father? Because you do love him, don't you dear?'

'Oh, I do, I do, I always will,' sobbed Antonia, unable to hold back her emotions any longer. Some of the children playing around them looked up, their eyes widening at the sight of their favourite librarian in tears. Their concerned parents tried to hush them, not quite sure what they should do. Some of them started to move away, not wanting to embarrass Antonia. But one parent had moved closer.

Absorbed in the old lady's story, Antonia had failed to notice that the young father she had stepped around on her way into the children's corner was now standing before her, his baby cradled in his right arm. His face was tired and thinner, etched with the unmistakable signs of suffering, and there were some threads of grey in the otherwise glossy black hair. But when he spoke to Antonia it was as though the library itself had faded away and she was alone with him in a grove of olive trees beneath a warm Mediterranean sky. The months and months of suffering, the pain of parting, were cancelled in that moment.

'Antonia, *ti amo*.'

'And I love you too, Lorenzo,' she cried. In the next instant she was caught in the curve of his free arm and felt the press of his lips against her own. She had never forgotten that delicious pressure but had never thought she would experience his kisses again. Thinking she must be dreaming again, she shut her eyes tight and then opened them, to see a little face framed with downy black hair looking up into her own out of familiar slate-grey eyes.

'Oh Lorenzo, he's adorable!' she cried, and lifted the little boy tremulously into her arms. He smiled and crowed, showing two new frilly front teeth. Antonia's heart went out to him in that moment.

'Meet Gianluca,' murmured Lorenzo in her ear.

'I am dreaming!'

'So come with me and we'll never wake up. You can guess

who his godmother is. She adores him.' Antonia looked down at the child, and then up into the face of the man she loved. Then she turned to the old Irishwoman in gratitude. Teresa Conroy, Lorenzo's own old nanny, was looking as pleased as punch, her face wreathed in smiles.

'Sure and didn't I know you'd still love my boy – he was so terrified it would be too late, and that you'd have moved him out of your life. That's why he wanted me to make sure for him first. And will you like the wee man, too?' she asked anxiously.

'I don't know how anyone could fail to love such a sweet little boy,' answered Antonia warmly, adding wistfully, 'and I never, ever stopped loving his father.'

'Give me that wee man here, then. He's a good wee walker now and doesn't need to carried everywhere, much as he likes it!' Teresa Conroy reached for the toddler, who went contentedly into her arms. Antonia felt his father's mouth once more against hers, gently taking possession again of what had always been his.

It was as if they were unaware of the whole world around them, this little family of man, woman, child and trusted old nurse were so completely absorbed in one another. Then a small cough interrupted them. Suddenly Antonia remembered where they were. Her colleagues and some of the readers were standing in a little group a discreet distance away. Lauren was sniffing and dabbing at her eyes with a crumpled handkerchief, and she was not the only one who was affected. Valerie was only pretending to look severe. Hands on hips, with one eyebrow raised, she addressed Antonia with what was meant to be a tone of authority but which did not quite come out that way.

'Miss Gray, as your boss I am instructing you to take the afternoon off. This behaviour is quite unsuitable for a library.' Then her voice changed as she added warmly, 'Oh Antonia, my dear, we're all so pleased for you. Now when do I get a chance to cuddle that lovely boy?'

Teresa Conroy insisted firmly on taking little Gianluca for a walk. 'Now you young people will have a lot to talk about. Gianluca and I have got plenty of new friends here, so off you two go and make up for lost time. After all, it's Gianluca's future that's at stake here too.'

Later that afternoon Antonia found herself as she had never dreamed she would be again, folded naked into her lover's arms in the delightful afterglow of their lovemaking. He was still covering her face with desperate kisses, as if to convince himself that all of this was for real.

'I have never, ever, been so happy,' she breathed.

'Nor I. I thought we were as deliciously happy as we could ever be, back there in Italy. But that doesn't even compare with what I feel now, finding you again after I thought I'd lost you forever! And this time, I'm never letting you go!' To emphasise his words, he squeezed her even more tightly to him.

'But how did all this happen?' She faltered, hardly daring

to ask, afraid of shattering the peace of that moment. After all they had suffered, Antonia had to know.

Lorenzo sighed, and his handsome face darkened with pain. 'Giselle lost interest in Gianluca before he was born, even more quickly than I'd thought she would. I worried about whether this was my fault, but I couldn't force myself to feel for her what I felt for you. I was prepared to do what she wanted, stick with her, pretend that we were the golden couple, for his sake. I thought we might manage it as she'd be away for work so much – she said she had no intention of changing that, and that other people could be hired to look after Gianluca.

'As Giselle's pregnancy went on, her dislike of our unborn child grew. She complained about him as if he were some alien being that had taken her over and was ruining her life deliberately. It was horrible for both of us, but I pleaded with her not to have an abortion. I just hoped that when she saw him her attitude would change. But when Gianluca was actually born, it was as if he had nothing to do with her, as if he hadn't been growing in her all that time. The nurses placed him on Giselle's body and I watched her, desperately willing her to put her arms around him, to soften a little. But no, nothing. I'll never forget it, as long as I live, the sight of that helpless little thing lying abandoned on his own mother's breast. She made no attempt to hold him even when he started to cry in real confusion and distress. When he tried to look for a feed – his instinct was so strong, even though he was only minutes old – she shrieked, "Take him away! I don't want him!" What I felt most in that moment was pity for my son and hate for his mother because she had rejected him.'

'Perhaps you are being too hard, Lorenzo. That might be post-natal depression. A lot of new mothers have ambivalent feelings about the baby.'

'I hoped that might be so, because then there might be something that could be done. But there wasn't. I asked all the specialists I could get to listen to me. Giselle wasn't despairing. She was simply not interested, except in complaining about what pregnancy had done to her figure. Enormous bills started to arrive from beauty salons, all of which I paid.

'But for all that, I had a glimmer of hope in the middle of all that pain. Some small part of me realised then that before too long Gianluca and I would be alone. The thought that there was a slim chance for you and me to be together again was almost painful to think about. What if I'd lost you already? And realistically, how could I ask you to accept another woman's child?'

'But I do!' cried Antonia. 'He's so beautiful, just like his father, and such a happy child. At least half of him is you, so how could I reject him?'

'My darling Antonia,' he murmured gently, 'take your time. I am divorcing Giselle. It'll cost me a bit, but that's the least of it. I believe she wants to marry a Swiss banker, twenty years older than her, and the man wants a trophy wife but not some other man's baby. But what if Giselle causes trouble for us later, or tries to interfere in how I bring up – I mean how we bring up Gianluca?'

'I'll stand by your side, Lorenzo. But you – or we – must think about what we tell Gianluca about Giselle. We must be scrupulously fair to her, whatever her reasons for doing what she did. He will have to know who his birth mother is. You talk about her causing trouble, or interfering. But what if one day she simply wants to be part of the life of her son? We cannot or should not stop her. None of this will be neat and tidy, because humans aren't like that. I'm going to do all I can to help you make it work, though.'

'You're right, of course you are. At the moment I can't see beyond the end of the divorce proceedings. To just be free to marry you and to make sure I can give my son the best life I can. I want you to know though that I've never stopped thinking about you, never stopped loving you all this time. But you, self-sufficient person that you are, you've rebuilt a life for yourself in spite of all the hurt you've suffered. How can you be so sure that you want me after all that and with all this baggage?'

'Lorenzo,' she answered slowly, 'I've never been so sure of anything. I've made a life for myself here, it's true, but then I've always had to manage. There was nobody to do it for me. But I've never stopped loving you, ever. Even if I'd wanted to, I couldn't have forgotten you. And I didn't want to. You were the best thing that ever happened to me. I couldn't cancel all that out. But now tell me how you found me.'

Lorenzo snuggled down in the little bed to pillow his head against her breasts before he spoke again. 'I had to do something quickly, to help my poor child. My own dear Nanny Conroy came to the rescue, all the way back from Ireland. She might have been retired a good while, but she never forgot her skills. She's a wise old counsellor as well. She planned how we would do this. She gave me back my sanity, my drive. I told her all about you, everything …'

'Everything?'

'Yes, including my appalling behaviour to you when I first met you. I didn't spare myself, Antonia, honestly. She calmed my fears, told me that there was no way you couldn't still love me. What convinced her was the way you left me, you see. Only someone who loved me as unselfishly as you did would have done what you did. Anyone else would have accepted the financial arrangements I was going to make for the care of my son and would have brushed aside the pain and guilt I would have felt at being parted from him. But of course, when Nanny Conroy arrived Giselle took off sharpish. She would have preferred some young au pair she could have bullied, but I wanted someone to care for my son, not someone who would become Giselle's personal skivvy. The atmosphere until she left felt so thick I thought I was almost physically wading through hate the whole time. We were living in Lausanne in a house she had inherited, and the feeling of pressure was sometimes so great I thought even the walls would crack. What a place to bring up a child! She complained all the time she was at home that we never saw anybody. I reminded her curtly that she never wanted to see her son, so we would certainly not be wasting time with anyone else. It was strange saying that, I remember. We'd known so many people, but it turned out that they were really fair-weather friends who only saw babies as getting in the way of fun. And besides, I felt I'd grown out of the life they represented. I went down to Gavedo with Gianluca and Nanny Conroy. Working with Paolo helped me feel better, and there was also my aunt. I knew she didn't like to come to Gavedo, so the three of us went to see her often. The villa could have been a real haven of peace for me, but my darling Antonia, I kept looking for you around every corner, expecting to find you strolling about those country paths, or bent over your computer in the library, working away. Then those people from Florence came, and I thought, and my aunt thought, that we might be able to lure you back that way. Together we did a bit of online sleuthing. You keep a very low profile on social media, I have to say. Only LinkedIn and you weren't giving much away there – only the vaguest of locations. I'm afraid that one of the ways we found you was that George fellow.'

'George!'

'Yes. I wish I hadn't had to mention him. I looked up

newspaper reports online of cases like his, and eventually found the one that fitted. His home town was mentioned, so I went there and found your old boss, Arthur. He was very protective of you, and quite rightly wouldn't tell me where you were. But eventually he picked up the phone to Valerie, and she said I should come here, and she'd take full responsibility. So here I am ...' His voice tailed away as he lifted his head and his mouth brushed hers.

'This is too good to be true,' she murmured.

'But it is true, my darling,' he replied, his mouth close to her ear as he nuzzled her. 'Let me show you how true it is, Antonia, my wife, mother of my child,' he continued, breaking off only to use his mouth in even more expressive ways.

She felt his unstoppable erection nudge against her with increasing urgency.

'Let me show you,' his voice dragged, thick with desire, and her legs parted gently to let him enter her again. When later they clung together in exhaustion, bodies flushed, she knew that all their suffering had been worthwhile. This was their destiny, and nothing could have changed that.

Chapter Eleven

Antonia stood in a pool of summer sunlight near the open window of the villa. The excited voices of the countess's staff drifted up to her from the ground floor, where they rushed around outside in a frenzy of activity.

Teresa Conroy clapped her hands together in admiration. 'Ah sure, you're a princess now and no mistake. Just look at you!'

Antonia smiled back at the two elderly ladies through the antique lace of the countess's mother's wedding veil, held on her curls by a coronet decorated with sweet, fresh lilies. The beautifully cut ivory silk dress, which showed off her neat curves to best effect, rustled as she moved towards them.

'Is it time?' she asked, in barely a whisper, unable to keep the emotion out of her voice. In the distance, as if answering her question, church bells began to peal.

There was a discreet knock at the door, and Teresa Conroy hurried to open it. Arthur Bennett stood there, beaming with pride and pleasure, spruced up in his best suit, which still just about fitted around his portly figure, a white carnation in his button hole.

'Now, are you quite sure about this, my dear girl? You know I'd never forgive myself if you'd changed your mind and I never gave you the chance to say so. Although I must say I think your choice is an admirable one.'

'Oh Arthur, I'm quite sure,' laughed Antonia. 'But it's so nice that you want to do all the right things!' She took the arm that he held out to her, and the little party descended the marble staircase and went out into the sunshine. Luigi jumped out from behind the wheel of a gleaming white limousine to open its doors for them.

'You look so serious, Luigi!' said Antonia.

He tipped his chauffeur's cap to her and smiled, then grasped Antonia's shoulders in his big hands and kissed her joyfully on both cheeks through her veil. At last the limousine was loaded up with its cargo, and Luigi drove them slowly through the stillness of the summer morning to the little country church where Lorenzo Quattromani would be awaiting his bride.

Antonia remembered that summer day as the one when the whole world seemed to be smiling. Children waved and shouted, people hung out of windows in the villages they passed through. Even the local dogs entered into the spirit of the day, running up and down and barking with excitement.

The steps of the little church were strewn with flowers, and Antonia walked slowly up them clinging tightly to Arthur Bennett's arm. Feeling as if she were moving in a dream, she passed through the doors of the ancient building and into the coolness within. The faces of the congregation turned to see her. Jane was there with Simon, emanating their joy of seeing their friend happy at last. Valerie looked round, catching Antonia's glance and smiling, as she had when she'd told Antonia she'd never find a worthy replacement for her. Old Alessio and the countess's other employees were there, to witness the marriage at last that marked the end of half a century of bad blood between the two factions of the great Quattromani family. The youngest member of the Quattromani family sat to one side of the altar, wearing a solemn expression, his little legs swinging because they could not reach the floor. Two little choir-boys, not much bigger than he was, sat with him, but Gianluca's round eyes were fixed on his father, whose shoulders fidgeted in his dark suit. The best man put his hand on Lorenzo's arm, trying to calm the groom's wedding nerves. Antonia did not recognise the man with Lorenzo straightaway. His trusted estate manager Paolo looked entirely different in his dark suit and vigorously polished shoes. Her own silk shoes trod on fragrant petals scattered along the aisle. Somehow she arrived at the altar and those extraordinary slate-grey eyes looked into hers.

'You came!' he whispered, and her nervousness vanished.

Three weeks later the Mercedes glided through the gates of the Gavedo estate. Rows of vines, already heavy with the year's harvest, flashed past Antonia's window.

'I can't wait to see Gianluca again!' she exclaimed. 'He's sure to have grown while we've been away. It's the only thing I regret about our honeymoon, not having him with us.'

'You mustn't regret anything about the time we've had,' her husband gently reproached her. 'And a honeymoon is a honeymoon.'

'Oh, I don't really mean it like that.' She stretched out languorously, thinking about the warm evenings, the soft lapping of the waters of the Adriatic Sea against the landing stage of the island in the Venetian lagoon, the long nights naked in the canopied bed of their exclusive little hotel. There was no doubt that lovemaking was different when you were married. It had that sweet and soothing sense of security. 'But I'm so happy to be home, too.' she added.

'If Gianluca has got bigger, it won't be the only surprise,' Lorenzo informed her mysteriously. As the car followed a curve in the road and Gavedo castle came into view, Antonia cried out in delight. The old fortress was half covered in scaffolding that swarmed with workmen. The air rang with the clang of tools and shouted instructions. Paolo stood in animated conversation, aided by plentiful gestures, with an oddly familiar female figure, also wearing overalls and a hard hat. Antonia could not place her for a minute, but then she burst out, 'Look, Lorenzo, there's Valerie!'

'Of course,' he answered. 'She's our partner in this

project. She has suggested Horizons as a working title, but of course the final say must be yours. After all, it was your idea – a sort of exchange programme. Young people can come here and work on the estate and earn their keep that way, and spend part of the time perhaps learning new skills in the castle's facilities.'

'Oh yes,' broke in Antonia excitedly, 'languages, computing, cooking, there's lots of things. It's another dream coming true.'

'With your organisational skills and enthusiasm, it's bound to succeed. This is going to be about other people seeing dreams come true too. Come on though, let's see our son first.'

Minutes later, Lorenzo Quattromani lifted his wife in his arms and carried her over the threshold of their home. A delighted Teresa Conroy put down her knitting and jumped up to greet them.

'My darling children,' she cried, and hugged them both tightly. 'It's lovely to see you both back home! You've just missed the wee feller,' she explained. 'He's gone down to the village with his godmother. She's come up once a week since you've been away and always takes him away for an hour or so. It always gives me a chance to put my feet up,' and she gestured towards her knitting, 'because I don't get much of a chance of that now that he's walking so well.'

'Oh, let's go and find him,' Antonia begged her husband.

'It'll not take long, just down to the village and back!'

'Of course, my darling. We'll be back soon, Nanny.'

The old countess and her godson were nowhere to be found in the village. Lorenzo eventually asked an old man sitting in the sun outside a bar if he had seen an old lady with a stick and a toddler any time that afternoon. The old man's face lit up with pleasure.

'Up there.' He gestured in the direction of the cemetery and the abandoned church.

They found Luigi's old car parked by the little churchyard gate. From where they stood, Antonia and Lorenzo could see clearly the two figures by the wall of the church.

'Let's not disturb them,' she whispered, 'We can wait for them here.'

The old countess's hand rested on the plaque. She seemed to be praying. Nearby, a dark-haired toddler sat still and quiet on a stone, watching her. Then he got unsteadily to his feet, as if he were still not quite confident about his legs, and took hold of the wreath that was lying beside him. It looked nearly as big as he was, but with an air of determination he pulled at it and finally managed to totter over to his godmother with it and tug at her skirt. She looked round, smiled at the little boy and kissed him. Together they placed the wreath against the wall, and Laura Quattromani kissed the plaque in farewell. Then she took Gianluca's small hand in her own and slowly she and the tiny boy made their way to where Antonia and her husband stood waiting for them.

About the Author

Kate Zarrelli is the romance and erotica pen-name of Katherine Mezzacappa. Kate is Irish but now lives in Carrara in Northern Tuscany, between the Apuan Alps and the Tyrrhenian Sea, with her Italian husband. She writes historical, erotic, feel-good and paranormal fiction, set all over Europe, and in her spare time volunteers with a used book charity of which she is a founder member. You can follow her on Facebook at Kate Zarrelli books or on Twitter @katmezzacappa.

ND - #0421 - 270225 - C0 - 203/127/11 - PB - 9781739117313 - Gloss Lamination